SPENCER'S BLUES

By

Andy Greenhalgh

ISBN 13: 978-1-6739-9028-7

'Sun going down, boy, dark gonna catch me here' –
Robert Johnson, *Crossroads Blues*

SPENCER'S BLUES

ACKNOWLEDGEMENTS

During the writing of this book I received advice and encouragement from a large number of people – too many to list here. There were some people, though, whose contribution significantly added to the content, detail or tone of the book and I would like to thank Jackie Anena, Nicola Alexis, Zein Al Oweis, Skye Bannister, Lexie Bourgeois, Susie Bishop, John Cagle (of the Georgia Bureau of Investigation), Steve Holland, Lynsey Metcalfe, Lindy Scopes, Red Szell and Kelly Watson.

(And my wife Gemma of course… for endless inspiration.)

Andy Greenhalgh

CHAPTER ONE

Every time Spencer Leyton cleared Immigration and Security and walked out into an airport arrivals hall, he always had the same fantasy. It happened once again here at Atlanta. He examined the line of drivers, each holding up the name of their passenger. There was Hernandez, Kriegl, Smith, but Spencer was taken with the middle-aged man holding up a sign saying 'Dr Morrison'. He stood for a moment, trying to summon up courage. The USA was, after all, the land of reinvention, so he could easily walk up to the driver and say 'Yes, that's me, I'm Dr Morrison.' He would be taken to a luxury hotel and asked to settle in for the night. In the morning a car would whisk him to an office block or conference centre where he would be invited to attend a round table discussion on global trends in the marketing of chicken salad sandwiches before giving a twenty-minute presentation called 'Mayonnaise – the question we cannot ignore.' Or perhaps Doctor Morrison was a wealthy plastic surgeon on his way back from a Florida golfing trip. Spencer would be driven out to one of the comfortable Atlanta suburbs to a gated community of lawn-sprinklers and security guards. His glamorous wife would open the door and any early bemusement at her husband's change in appearance would be dispelled by the explanation that he had been doing a surgical makeover on himself. There would be a dry martini and then a few hours passionate sex – something that Spencer had not experienced for as long as he could remember.

Reason prevailed, and he greeted the man holding a sign saying, 'Dr Spencer Leyton'. Walt Hite was, like Spencer, in his early forties. Unlike Spencer, he was possessed of a confident easy charm. A good-looking man with a full head of dark hair, he wore chinos, a plaid shirt, Tom Ford sunglasses and a jacket that looked casual but expensive. Spencer's outfit, by contrast, was looking a little tired. As was the man wearing it. He was of average height and slim build, with light brown hair swept back from his forehead. A man of unremarkable looks whose life-style choices had made him appear a little older than his years.

Walt's handshake was of the bone-cracking variety.

'Anything you want, just call Walt,' he said with a broad smile. 'How about we get a drink?'

'Can I smoke in a bar here?'

'You can burst into flames if you like.'

Crossing the car-park on an early Autumn evening Spencer was struck by the residual warmth of the day. Suddenly he wasn't in England any more.

****

If someone says, 'Do you want a job that involves tap-dancing through a mine-field?' the reasonable person thinks about it for an almost indescribably short time and then says no. When Spencer was offered the job, he should have thought about it for an almost indescribably short time and then he should have said no. But being Spencer, things did not work out quite like that.

'It's all part of an exchange programme; you go there, and an American academic comes to a college somewhere here. It's being funded by an endowment in the States. You would be over there for half a term, or semester, as they say. Actually, it's eight weeks in all.' Spencer's manager, Jane, had explained it all to him, 'That would be fine with us. We can put you on sabbatical. We can share your classes here amongst the other teachers. I think it will do you good. It will be a challenge for you.'

It will also mean you don't have to pay my salary for eight weeks, thought Spencer.

'And the college you're going to – well, it sounds just your sort of place. It's not one of your stuffy private schools full of over-privileged brats…'

So it was full of under-privileged brats, thought Spencer.

'It's in a vibrant part of the town…'

'Vibrant' was often a code-word for dangerous. He was starting to realise why no one else in the faculty had put themselves forward for the job.

'Anyway, here's a complete job description. Let me know what you think in a couple of days.'

Back in his office, Spencer saw that the pile of papers on the desk had at last toppled over onto the chair. He really needed to get round to sorting that lot out, he thought to himself as he scooped them all up and dumped them onto the floor. They joined the pile of papers that had gone through the same transition the week before. He plumped down in the chair to read the job description. The first paragraph was fairly predictable, a version of the university's mission statement, full of the usual hieroglyphics about the interface of methodology and culture, the empowerment of the dashboard of inclusivity. It was only when he turned the page to the section on remuneration that he began to perk up. His stint would earn him considerably more than he would earn in London, and he had already been assured that any payment would be tax free. What would be keeping him here anyway? It was nearly four years since his wife Sarah had thrown him out and he had given up all hope of getting back together with her, and although he generally saw his children every two weeks, he was starting to think that it was more for his benefit than for theirs. He would miss them – he would miss them very much – but they could always Skype. And anyway, he would not be away for long.

Professionally, he really did need a challenge. The general chaos in his personal life had almost cost him his job two years earlier, and since then as a teacher he felt he had been treading water. He knew that he had become stale, teaching the same topics in the same way with lessening enthusiasm.

What would he be leaving behind? He had some good friends here in London, but he had not been in a sexual relationship for months – and too much of his time was spent in the pub.

Spencer picked up a blank sheet of paper from the floor, drew a line down the centre and on one side wrote 'Reasons to go' and on the other 'Reasons to stay'

Under 'Reasons to go' he wrote: More money/ New experience/ Hot weather/ Invigorate my teaching/ Look good on the cv. Under 'Reasons to stay' he wrote: Vague designs on the new woman in HR.

What if the challenge really were a challenge? He had taught some difficult students in London; what if he were to encounter much more difficult ones over there? He had taught lazy students, manipulative students, students who could lie as easily as breathing in and out. What if this were to be straight from the frying pan and into the fire? He dismissed the thought. 'What are you, Spencer?' he enquired aloud, 'Man or mouse?' What was that squeaking noise?

He looked again at 'Reasons to go'. Why on earth could he not write down the main reason why he knew it was a good idea to get away from London? Was he still, after all this time, in denial?

Spencer read the job description. It seemed that his only duties would be to deliver a series of seminars under the title 'Shakespeare's Tragedies and Romances for the 21st century: A British View'. This would surely not be too difficult. He loved Shakespeare; he always had. He loved Shakespeare for his stories, his characters, his use of language, but mainly for his matchless understanding of human nature. For Spencer, Shakespeare's Complete Works could be seen almost as a secular Bible. Shakespeare seemed to understand the human condition instinctively. He was a man who had never walked the corridors of power, yet had a consummate knowledge of politics. He was a man who had never left the shores of England (who thought Florence was a port city), yet had written plays that had been translated into almost every language and performed in almost every country. Certainly Spencer would never claim that every single one of Shakespeare's plays was an undying masterpiece, but it seemed that he could choose his list of plays himself. He could swerve the three or four plays that he found tiresome. Who wanted to plough through King John?

He did a little research online. Pellier University was a state-supported, liberal arts college in the town of Merganserville, about fifty miles outside Atlanta, Georgia. Merganserville was a community of some 15,000 people. When he tried to find a little more beyond the university website, some worrying details came up. The most notable recent event was a rally against police violence and racism. It was a peaceful demonstration broken up by dogs and tear gas.

He found a YouTube video of a former student denouncing certain 'fascistic and homophobic members of faculty'. On one of the student forums there was a long and puzzling discussion about a comedian called Dave Whittier being banned from campus for purveying 'cis-gendered shit'. There was talk of 'trigger warnings' and 'safe spaces', and a host of other preoccupations that rarely reared a head at his college in London. Tiny alarm bells were going off in Spencer's mind but, as he said to himself again, eight weeks was not long.

Spencer accepted the job. Two weeks and a flurry of emails later, his visa and flight were arranged. An apartment on campus and a rental car would be ready for him…

****

Spencer poured himself into Walt's Mercedes and they left the airport. They shot up a ramp and onto a four-lane highway. The city opened out below him. Walt drove at speed, furiously overtaking on both outer and inner lanes. Scarily, every other driver seemed to be doing the same thing.

This was only Spencer's second trip to the US. Seven years earlier he had spent a week in Las Vegas during August. The temperature had reached 40 Celsius every day. The only answer to the bludgeoning heat was to sleep all day and spend the nights drinking and gambling, often simultaneously. He was generally wise enough to play poker against people who were more drunk than he was, and in the early hours of the morning these people were not hard to find. He would get to bed at dawn and rise in the middle of the afternoon with a fistful of money-off vouchers: *Try our 4lb Monster Waffle – just 25 cents at Lucky Sam's Coffee House at the Venetian Hotel: Voted Best Coffee House at the Venetian Hotel.* He would attend an All-You-Can-Eat Buffet and take them at their word, and then produce a voucher to give him free admission to a late-afternoon comedy show (*Voted Best Late-Afternoon Comedy Show*) where he would be entertained by ageing comedians with the dress-sense of Liberace and the politics of Joseph Goebbels. It was, in fact, possible to live in Vegas virtually for free – as long as you did not gamble. But if you did not gamble, why were you in Vegas? At the time, Spencer's life had revolved round gambling but even for him a week was more than enough.

They arrived in the city of Atlanta and stopped at a large, brightly lit bar.

'This is a pretty good place for eye candy,' said Walt as they walked in, 'and I am being gender-neutral.'

At the bar, Spencer gulped down two pints of craft beer and immolated half a pack of cigarettes while Walt filled him in on life at Pellier University. He explained that he was a lecturer in the combined school of English and Theatre studies, and that his specialism was the modern American Theatre. He said that he had been there for the last three years and basically liked it pretty much. He added that he was almost the only heterosexual male teacher in the Arts Faculty.

'How about you?'

'Me? Er… well, I was married until a little while ago.'

'Married? That don't mean a thing! You can be married to a man nowadays. The way things are going, by next year you'll be able to marry any of the higher primates.'

'Oh, yeah, right. I was married, but not to a man. I was married to… well, to a woman actually. Er… how about you?'

'No,' said Walt, 'I've never been married. Came close a couple of times, but saw sense at the last minute. So yes, I'm free and single, and will probably stay that way. He raised his glass, grinning, "America – the Land of the Free."'

Spencer laughed, 'You know what the Brits say, don't you? In America you are free to do what you are told.'

'Oh, well, I get that. Parts of this country are deeply conservative and conformist – and that includes the South, of course.'

Spencer was feeling weary. He gazed around the bar. As Walt had suggested, most of the customers were young and good looking. They were mostly dressed in casual but spotlessly clean outfits. There was none of the boho chic he was used to in London. The big contrast, though, with any of his local bars in Clapham, was that, of the fifty or sixty customers, every single one was white.

As in many American bars, there were a dozen TV screens, each showing a different sports event. Walt was taking a keen interest in a college football game.

'Is that your team playing?' asked Spencer.

'Er, not exactly… Let's just say I have a financial interest…' Walt chuckled to himself.

'You've got a bet on it? Is that legal here?'

'It is absolutely not legal. The gambling laws in Georgia are about the strictest in the whole country.'

'So you're betting with an illegal bookie? Isn't that a bit risky?'

Walt laughed. 'Isn't gambling supposed to be risky? I thought that was the whole point.' He took a drink. 'Do you bet, Spencer?'

'Not any more. I used to, but, well… It all went a bit too far, if you know what I mean.'

'What did you bet on?'

Spencer laughed, 'Everything: horses, sports… Poker was my main thing. But then, you see, I broke the one rule of gambling – don't bet more than you can afford to lose.'

'You say it went too far… Do you mean you were hooked on it? Sorry Spencer, I've only just met you, I shouldn't really…'

'No that's okay. I'll talk about it with anyone.' Spencer thought for a little while. 'Yes, I was addicted to it. Of course some people would say that I will always be addicted to it: you know, like you never stop being an alcoholic – you are just an alcoholic who doesn't drink anymore.'

'But back then you were a gambling junkie?'

'I don't really like the word 'junkie'. That means someone addicted to heroin, and compulsive gambling is not the same as physical dependence, not at all.' He paused, glass in hand, 'When I stopped… when I stopped, well, I didn't have physical withdrawal symptoms. The problem was filling my time; suddenly there was a hole in my life that I had to fill.'

'So how did you fill it?'

'I didn't. I mean it's been over two years since I stopped, and the desire is still there. It's like an itch... an itch I must not scratch.' He took a swig of beer, 'Look, I would rather you kept this to yourself…'

'You're secret's safe with me, buddy.'

'Well, you see it's one of the reasons that I took this job. Quite simply, I wanted to get away from London. Recently… these last few weeks… the need to gamble has been coming back to me and London is a bad place for a compulsive gambler. There's a betting shop on every high street. If I go into the centre of town, I can spend the night drifting between casinos. Well, I knew it would be different here in Georgia.'

'It is. Believe me.'

'The danger, of course, is that you replace one addiction with another.' Spencer held up his glass, 'so I'm careful with this stuff now.'

'One day at a time, eh? You can be addicted to almost anything – did you know that? Maybe your next addiction will be sex.'

'Well at least that's cheap.'

'Are you kidding?' Walt laughed, 'It's the most expensive of all. Let's get back on the road.'

It was dark when they left the bar, and Spencer slept for most of the hour's journey to Merganserville. Walt took him to his accommodation, which was a smart apartment in a modern, three-storey block on the edge of the Pellier campus. Spencer fell onto the bed and slept in his clothes. In his dream he was in Vegas, officiating at a wedding where Walt was marrying Liberace.

****

'Do I really need a car? I seem to be living right on campus.'

It was nine the next morning and Walt was driving Spencer to pick up his rental car.

'Look Spencer, this ain't London. It's a small town in Georgia, and there is hardly any public transportation. You'll need a car just to get to the store. Besides, you'll be wanting to get out of Merganserville to see the sights, won't you?'

Spencer was not sure which sights were being recommended. They pulled into the car park of the rental car showroom.

'Have you seen *Vanishing Point*, Walt?'

'Yep. Great movie. The car is a 1970 Dodge Challenger with a 440 engine.'

'What's a 440 engine?'

'About equivalent to 7 litres,' said Walt, laughing.

'My God. What does Steve McQueen drive in *Bullit*?'

'That's a 1968 Ford Mustang.'

'Can I get something like that?'

'I already booked the car. There it is – outside the office.'

Walt pointed at the car. It was a Nissan. In beige.

'Oh. Right. Thanks.'

Spencer's apartment was small but comfortable and very quiet. He was not aware of his neighbours and wondered if the block was reserved for visiting foreign academics. There was a living room, a bedroom, a bathroom, a kitchen and a broom cupboard. His living room window looked onto the campus; his bedroom window looked onto the perimeter road. He made a list of the provisions he would need to buy, which did not take long because he had no intention of cooking anything more elaborate than tea and toast. Why did Americans not use electric kettles?

Spencer's office was situated in the Josef H Schweinsteiger Building, part of the Sinead O'Keefe Center for the Performing Arts. His seminars were to be held in the Dolores del Durango Arts Studios, which were in another wing of the campus, part of the Mikhail Shafranovich Cultural Center. It was becoming clear that much of the campus only existed because of the generosity of a few wealthy individuals who really wanted their names to live on.

He had been in email contact with Louisa Wilson, who taught Theatre Arts. Meeting her, Spencer was pleased to see that she was an attractive woman in her thirties, with sleek dark hair falling to her shoulders. She wore a well-cut jacket over a bright blouse. Spencer was starting to feel a little underdressed. He introduced himself.

'I just luurve your accent, Spencer.'

He refrained from the obvious rejoinder that actually *she* was the one with the accent. He felt he was in safe hands: Louisa was brisk and efficient, but there was a warmth about her that he found reassuring.

'Spencer, just to confirm: the title of your course is: *Shakespeare's Tragedies and Romances for the 21st Century: A British view.* You'll be giving a seminar every Tuesday and Thursday morning. There will be an introductory seminar and then you'll discuss two different plays each week, if that's okay.'

'Yes, that's the plan. Do you know my students? Ever taught them?'

'Yep. This is a small school. I know all your students. They are okay, but there's quite a range in terms of ability – and commitment, actually.'

'Well, I'm used to that. What do you teach yourself?'

Louisa chuckled, 'As head of department I seem to have ended up as Jill-of-All-Trades. At the moment I'm teaching Acting, and I'm teaching a course on Applied Theatre, but I've taught Classical Greek Theatre in the past. And Restoration Comedy… the list goes on, frankly. So, just to clarify: you'll be teaching two seminars each week…'

'Yes.'

'… and you'll have two weeks off. You will have Thanksgiving week off, and the week after that the students will be in rehearsal, although we would appreciate any input on their productions.'

'That's fine with me. What productions do you have in mind?'

'There are two Shakespeare plays to be directed and performed by the students and, as I say, we would be happy if you were able to sit in on some rehearsals.'

'Which plays?'

Louisa consulted her computer, '*Romeo and Juliet* and *Merchant of Venice*. Just small-scale studio productions, you understand… ' Louisa chuckled to herself. '*Not* the sort of thing you might see around Lye-sesster Square'

'Er… yes… My workload is not what you'd call punishing…'

'Hold your horses,' smiled Louisa, 'there's something else you need to know. Seminars here normally last for seventy-five minutes, but we want the students to have an immersive British experience…'

'So should I dress up as a Beefeater?'

Louisa looked blank for a moment. Spencer asked himself why he should assume that an American academic would know what a Beefeater was.

'The dress code for staff is smart casual' said Louisa, with a nervous smile. 'Er… as I was saying, we want the students to get their money's worth from you, so your seminars will each last for three hours.'

Spencer was more than a little taken aback. 'Have you told the students?'

'Yes.'

'And how did they react?'

'Well … let's just say they were surprised.'

'Er… okay. Is there anything else you'd like me to do?'

'Sure. We'd like you to take an interest in everything that's happening on campus.'

'That's fine with me.'

'If you're not busy, could you come to the campus comedy club tonight?'

'That sounds great.'

'I'll meet you at 7.30 at the J. Horace Handwinder studio theatre.'

That evening, as they found their seats in the theatre, Spencer examined the students sitting around him. There were some in the conventional American campus uniform of scrubs or sportswear, with numerous tracksuits emblazoned with the name of the college football team, 'The Pellier Peregrines'. There were a number of shaved heads and piercings: evidence for Spencer that some tribal loyalties had survived the homogenisation of social media. He thought back to his own student days: he had flirted with post-punk and grunge before accepting that he didn't like the music and looked ridiculous in the clothes. By the time of his final undergraduate year he had settled into whatever tribe it was that listened to Delta Blues and bought all their clothes at charity shops.

Since Pellier was a Liberal Arts college, Spencer was not surprised that the audience for the comedy show was overwhelmingly female. What did surprise him (having been to London comedy clubs) was that all the performers were female too. The humour was largely observational and was greatly enjoyed by the young audience, but for Spencer the observations could have been coming from a different planet. There were jokes about women dating women, jokes about navigating drunken men at frat parties, jokes about internet memes, jokes about TV shows of which he had never heard. What on earth was Cosplay?

Louisa chuckled her way through the first half, and at the interval turned to him with an apologetic smile, 'I don't think this is quite your sort of thing, is it Spencer? Are you the wrong gender for most of the jokes?'

'Wrong gender, wrong sexual inclination, wrong generation, wrong nationality.' He smiled at Louisa, 'Or maybe I just don't have a sense of humour.'

He had a sense that his time in Merganserville might prove to be a bumpy ride.

****

Spencer was on his way to his first seminar when Walt bounded up.

'How's it going?' Walt demanded, slapping Spencer on the shoulder.

'Well, I'm on my way to my first class so, y'know, I'm a little nervous…'

'Oh, you'll be fine, don't worry.'

'I went to the campus comedy club last night…'

'You did *what*? Are you crazy?'

'I had no idea how uncomfortable I would feel. I mean some of them were pretty good, quite funny in their way but…'

'You were part of a minority for once.'

'Well, yeah, I guess so. Out of my comfort zone, y'know.'

'Because you are, after all, a middle-aged heterosexual cis-gendered white man…'

'Exactly.' Spencer smiled.

'I haven't been to a comedy night here since the Dave Whittier thing – you know about that?'

'I think I heard something…'

'I really don't know why they booked him. I saw him in a club in Atlanta a couple of years ago, and I could have told them there would be problems… Put it this way: he came out on stage and told a string of anti-gay jokes. He was going on about dykes and faggots and God knows what. Within a few minutes he had the whole goddamn crowd on their feet screaming at him. So since then – get this – they have a student committee to vet any comedians before they book them. Comedians have to post an extract from their act on YouTube, and anyone who doesn't fit in with the committee's viewpoint doesn't get a booking.'

'Who elects the committee?'

'The only ones who bother to vote are the people who are on the committee already.' There was a glint in Walt's eye, 'Look, I'll tell you what, old buddy. On Friday I'll take you to a place where you'll fit right in. You won't be outside your comfort zone or any other zone. Yep, you'll just be one of the crowd. See you Friday, if not before.'

Spencer walked over to the seminar rooms wondering exactly what he was in for. There were ten students, eight of them women. There was also a striking ethnic mix. It was a 9am seminar, and some of the students looked as though they'd just got out of bed. In fact, some of the students had indeed just got out of bed. Only three hours to go, thought Spencer.

First he asked the students to put their mobile phones away, then he talked for a while about Shakespeare's life, about the themes of the plays and about modern critical response. He was just starting on Shakespeare in performance when one of the students raised a hand. It was Mary, a tall young woman at the back of the group. With her scrubbed face, her hair pulled back, and her Pellier University hooded top not quite concealing her pyjamas, Mary did not look like a morning person. Mary did not look as if she was happy to be there. Mary did not look as if she would be particularly happy anywhere.

'Professor…'

'Oh, call me Spencer, please.'

Spencer gave his most friendly and encouraging smile. It was, after all, the first student contribution of the entire term.

'Professor… can I go to the bathroom?'

Spencer's smile froze to rictus. This was a crucial moment: either he stamps his authority on the class or he kneels down in surrender.

'We will be taking a break in ten minutes, so if you could hang on till then?'

Mary glowered at him.

Spencer was starting to describe the physical circumstances of Shakespeare's theatre when Mary raised her hand again.

'Professor…?'

'Please call me Spencer.'

'Professor, why are we bothering with Shakespeare anyway?'

'Sorry?'

'What's it got to do with us? I mean he died about a thousand years ago, so how can it have anything to do with what's going on now?'

'Well it's 400 years, actually, but your question is certainly germane.'

'It's *what*? German?'

'It's germane. It's a relevant question. The point is this: Shakespeare is both of his time and out of his time. He is both Elizabethan and modern. A classic writer is re-invented in every age. Look, let's take the play we are going to be studying next week. Othello deals with race, sexual jealousy… how we use people for our own ends… I am sure you will agree that these themes are still alive today.'

'Professor…?

'Spencer.'

'Professor, can I go to the bathroom now?'

Like the French at Agincourt, like Richard at Bosworth, Spencer tasted the inevitability of defeat.

'Yes Mary. Let's take a fifteen-minute break.'

Spencer spent the break trying to find somewhere to smoke. He left the building and read a large sign saying that smoking was absolutely forbidden on campus everywhere, except in the DSA. He approached a young man who was quite clearly a student.

'Excuse me,' said Spencer,' but where can I find the DSA?'

'The what?'

'The Designated Smoking Area.'

'Didn't know we had one.'

Spencer walked into the gardens. He spoke to a middle-aged gardener in overalls and straw hat who was burning dead vegetation in an incinerator.

'Excuse me,' said Spencer, 'but do you know where I can find the Designated Smoking Area?'

'What the fuck do you want to smoke for?'

'What?'

'I gave up twenty years ago and that's when my life began.'

'Yes, well...'

'My father died because of smoking. My brother died because of smoking. I had cousins who were killed by smoking. It damn near wiped out my whole family. My buddy Dave has just gone down with emphysema so why the fuck do you want to smoke?'

Spencer was edging away, 'Well, thanks, but...'

'Throw them in the incinerator.'

'What?'

'Throw them in the incinerator and you ain't never gonna smoke again.'

Spencer ran for it.

'In twenty years' time you'll thank me like your best friend,' the man shouted after him.

Spencer turned the corner and ran into a young woman in a Pellier Peregrines track suit.

'Er... do you know where I can find the Designated Smoking Area?'

'Oh, you mean the Hiram J. Fishburne Designated Smoking Area.'

'Really?'

'It's right over the other side of campus, by the front gate. It's about ten minutes' walk.'

'Ten minutes? Oh my God.'

Spencer had to get back to the classroom. His route had described a semi-circle. He realised that the quickest way back would be if he went by the perimeter road. Breathing heavily, he jogged along the sidewalk. Cars were parked along the road. Spencer stopped short.
On a blue SUV was a fender sticker with the confederate flag and the slogan 'Make America White Again.'

He walked slowly for the rest of the way back to the class.

CHAPTER TWO

In the second half of the seminar, Spencer started by asking the students to put their mobile phones away. Then he opened up a general discussion on why Shakespeare is still relevant in the twenty-first century. It crawled along for an hour before Dani spoke up. Dani was a young blonde woman with big blue eyes. Spencer had a sense of a good figure hiding underneath her over-sized sweater. She twisted her fingers round a pen as she talked.

'The thing is, Professor, it just gets back to the same old problem.'

Spencer noticed instantly that Dani did not speak with a local accent.

'You're not from…?'

'I grew up in Chicago,' said Dani abruptly, closing the matter and turning the key.

'You see Professor, what's relevant to you is not really relevant to me, or to most of the people in this room.'

'Er…'

'Shakespeare was a man, wasn't he? His plays were performed by men – even the female roles – and his patrons were men, and most of his audience were men, at a time when most women were not taught to read, and…'

'Well most men weren't taught to read either, and as I recall it one of his patrons was Queen Elizabeth the First …'

'But that's just it.' Dani was starting to sound exasperated, 'It's not a question of gender so much as a question of, like, cultural values. Queen Elizabeth was part of a patriarchal culture and in becoming a head of the state she turns into a kind of honorary man. I mean, like, language itself is a male creation. Shakespeare's pre-occupation with, well with power and status and warfare – they are all male pre-occupations.' She would make brief eye-contact with Spencer and then her glance would flick away. 'Can't you see that women are bored with the literary canon, not because of its merits but because of the values underlying it? There is always this assumption that male writers represent the pinnacle of literary achievement…'

Dani tailed off and stared out of the window.

'Good… well, er… does anyone else have an input here? Er… Mark?'

Mark was wearing a Pride badge and a T-shirt with a picture of James Dean on it. Mark smiled at Spencer and said nothing. Spencer asked the students to put their mobile phones away.

'Right…look, er… Dani… I really think that Shakespeare can meet us halfway, whoever we are. We all have our baggage. I'm a white heterosexual man in early middle age. To some extent that shapes my attitudes, but I honestly don't think it makes it easier for me to appreciate

Shakespeare. I've always felt that his appeal is genuinely universal. You see, he wrote nearly all of his plays with the intention of selling tickets to a mass audience. I really don't see why his work can't speak to women just as much as to men.' Pleased with himself, Spencer sat back and smiled.

Dani replied, averting her eyes, 'Professor, I am happy to read books written by men, but Virginia Woolf will speak to my experience more than Henry James and life is too short for Beowulf.'

Spencer asked the students to put their mobile phones away and started again, staring at his students' faces, examining them for any tiny sense that he was winning them over. 'I think what it all comes down to is empathy. That is the quality that marks us out as human beings, and that is what Shakespeare has in abundance. He could put himself into the mind of every type of person, irrespective of gender or social class, because ultimately we are all individuals with our foibles and frailties that may or may not be representative of a group identity. So Shakespeare can take on the character of a medieval Scottish warlord, but can also take on the character of a lesbian from Colorado – If he had ever heard of Colorado, that is. Or lesbians, come to that.' He paused. What the fuck was he talking about? 'Well, I want you to read Othello for Thursday's class and I'll just take a few minutes now to sketch in some of the main themes.'

Mary had her hand up again. 'Professor, can I go to the bathroom?'

'But the class finishes in ten minutes.'

'It's a woman's problem, Professor: I am sure you'll understand.'

****

On Wednesday morning Spencer was due to meet with Louisa to discuss their plans for the term's work. Spencer had breakfast at a local diner and, reflecting that he had seen almost nothing of Merganserville, he took a roundabout route back to campus.

Many of the buildings in the university area seemed to date back to the nineteenth century, and the streets were, by American standards, quite narrow. As was to be expected of a neighbourhood near a college, there were any number of affordable restaurants. There was a Korean place, a Chinese place, several places serving different versions of Mexican food, and a couple of traditional 'Mom and Pop' diners where the waitresses might have been the grandmothers of the customers – and in some cases actually were. There was a menu displayed outside one of them: Spencer wondered what 'Collard Greens' might entail, and were they named after someone called Collard?

Walking a little further away from the university, he turned down a side street and noticed that some of the buildings were badly in need of repair. He wondered who lived there. Suddenly he became aware of a police siren and the sound of chanting, but could not make out what was being said. He turned a corner and walked towards the noise. There were police cars blocking the entrance to a small park. Inside were a group of perhaps fifty people chanting 'Pull it Down!' There were placards with slogans such as 'No to Hate' and 'No to Racism'. The protestors were grouped around a circle of police officers – all of them in riot gear – who were guarding a statue at the centre of the park. Spencer made his way round the police cars to move closer and realised that the statue depicted the Confederate general Robert E. Lee. The protestors mostly appeared to be students; he recognised three of them from his own class.

Suddenly, a scuffle broke out just in front of the police line. Spencer did not see how it began, but at once there were flailing arms, screams of pain and shouts of anger. The police line surged forward. Protesters were on the ground. For a moment, it looked as though a full-scale riot would break out. Horrified, Spencer shrank away. 'This is not my fight.' Did he just say that aloud? He ran from the park, stumbling over a homeless man sitting by the gate. Unsteady on his feet, Spencer walked back to campus, the squeal of an ambulance siren growing behind him. He sat for a while on a bench, trying to gather his thoughts. What the hell had he walked into?

Spencer met Louisa on campus at the Theodore Galapagos Coffee Lounge and explained to her what he'd just seen.

'I know,' said Louisa, 'I've just heard about it.' She looked shaken, 'One of the students has been taken to the hospital. The university security staff is talking to the police. They're trying to find out what happened.'

'Will there be some kind of enquiry? I mean, if people were hurt…?'

'Oh, there will be an enquiry, but whether it will achieve anything is a different matter. You see, there are some police officers who just seem to do what they want. Nobody is taking charge anymore and some of the local cops shouldn't be allowed anywhere near that protest at the statue. The combination of dark skins and political dissent seems to be too much for some of them. My God…' She drifted away for a moment. 'The statue has been there over a hundred years, but the trouble started when some right-wing groups began to use it as a rallying point. Then we had a speaker on campus saying that the Civil War was caused by disputes over taxation rather than by slavery and the whole thing blew up. We've had the Wednesday morning protest going on for the last three weeks. Things escalated a few days ago when Parnell Prince got involved.'

'Parnell Prince? Sounds like a 1970s porn star. Does he have floppy hair and a moustache?'

'I don't know. He does everything online. Very few people know what he looks like, so there are all kinds of rumours going about that he's a German aristocrat, or a dwarf, or a woman.'

'Or all three, I suppose.'

'Whoever he is, he's a white supremacist spokesman. He's thought to be active in various different groups and a kind of mystique has grown up around him, precisely because he remains invisible. That's one of the problems with the internet: one deranged individual can sit in his bunker sending out hate and he can give the impression that he is the leader of a mass movement.'

'So, what's he been doing, er… Porno Prince?'

Louisa giggled despite herself, 'He's been condemning the protest – in the most vile terms of course.'

'I know I'm just a visitor here and I don't really understand the background, but I'm not sure that pulling down the statue is the way to deal with it,' said Spencer.

Louisa nodded, 'Have you been to Vienna?' she said, 'There's a square called Judenplatz and on one of the walls is a medieval plaque glorifying a pogrom against the Jews. People could have asked for that to be torn down, but instead they commissioned Rachel Whiteread to build a huge memorial opposite it. The memorial is for the victims of the Holocaust. So it's not ignoring anti-Semitism; it's providing a response.'

Spencer gave a slight shudder. 'Well I'm glad none of this involves me. I don't really want one of those cops cracking my head open.'

After twenty minutes discussing their plans for the term they laid their papers aside. Spencer smiled, 'I went for breakfast this morning at the diner opposite the front entrance to campus.'

'Yes,' said Louisa, 'Loretta's Luncheonette.'

'Well could you speak to them? What they are doing in there is unconstitutional.'

'How on earth can it be unconstitutional?'

'They gave me something called biscuits and gravy. Well, first of all you have to understand that to an Englishman a biscuit is a crisp pastry to be served in the afternoon with a cup of tea, and gravy is a sauce served with mashed potato by a cook who has run out of ideas. So to be offered – at breakfast, mark you – balls of dough swimming in white gloop, well that qualifies as cruel and unusual punishment, and that is against the eighth Amendment of the American constitution.'

'Spencer, how long will it take me to get used to the British sense of humour?'

'A long time, and it probably isn't worth it.'

Spencer drank some coffee and asked, 'How do you get on with Walt?'

'Oh, fine… I mean, he does the unreconstructed man act a bit too much, but that's what it is – an act.'

'So why does he feel the need to put on an act?'

'Well… the department is very female-dominated, and I think he feels vulnerable. It's never easy being in a minority of any kind.'

'He's taking me out somewhere Friday evening. He hasn't told me where.'

'Probably an Elvis impersonator show. He's a big fan. Do you like that kind of thing?'

'The early stuff – Sun Records and all that. I like the blues.'

'You do? Well that gives me an idea for next week.' She was thoughtful for a moment. 'Spencer, I should tell you that Walt helped me when I first came here two years ago. I was not in a good place and he… yeah, he's a good guy...' She dropped her eyes.

'I know it's none of my business, but…'

'No, it's okay, I 'm happy to talk about it.' She stared down at her cup. 'I grew up in Atlanta and I married the boy next door – literally. I went on to be a college lecturer and Robert joined the police. Atlanta is no more dangerous than other cities in the USA, but he was unlucky. He kept getting involved in really scary situations and then finally he was shot in the leg.'

'Did he have to give up his job?'

'He wanted to carry on… but I told him I couldn't take it anymore. The day he handed in his resignation he was killed by a drunk driver.'

'Oh my God…'

There was silence as Louisa gazed out of the window. Finally she spoke, 'I just didn't want to be in Atlanta anymore. I felt that the place was cursed. A job came up here and so I moved to Merganserville. It took me a long time to come back to myself and Walt really helped me. He was just prepared to listen to me, you know?'

'Don't you find that those guys who come over as very macho are often very sensitive underneath?'

'Well, Robert was a bit like that. Old-fashioned, I guess.'

'Do you think Brits are different?'

'I haven't met that many, but you know the joke: 'Is that guy metrosexual or just European?''

'Walt said he was the only heterosexual male teaching in the Arts Faculty…'

'Oh, that's Walt's idea of a joke, but yeah… even today it's probably not that easy to be open about yourself here in the South. This is not San Francisco. Maybe Liberal Arts colleges offer something of a safe haven… I don't know.'

'Louisa, can I ask you something?

'Of course.'

'My first seminar this morning. It wasn't quite what I was expecting.'

'Are the students less diligent than the ones you're used to?'

'No, no, it's not that... They seem bright, and certainly some of them are prepared to join in the discussion. It's just that everything seems to be seen through the prism of identity politics, and that's just not my approach. For me

Shakespeare is about our communality; not what divides us.'

'Well, it's not as if we encourage them to see everything in terms of their own group, but so much modern critical analysis comes from that approach. I suppose even people as young as these students are aware of how the discourse was dominated for so long by Dead White Men. I mean, in that sense, something still has to be redressed.'

'Do I have to redress it?'

'All you have to do is inspire them. The most important thing a teacher has is passion. If you're passionate about Shakespeare, some of that will rub off.' She paused for a moment. 'Also – and I say this with respect – you should try to understand where they're coming from, and try to value their desire for something new.'

Spencer stared miserably at his coffee. 'I've got to be honest. I don't think I inspired them much today. I think some of them were bored.'

'Okay. Look Spencer, it really is early days. I don't think you should lose heart.' Louisa thought for a moment. 'Can I make a suggestion?'

'Yes... I mean I'll try anything.'

'If I'm teaching any kind of dramatic literature, I usually break the seminar format at some stage and get them up on their feet acting it out.'

'Well of course I teach acting back home and I do have some acting students in the class...'

'Then why not give it a try? There's really nothing to lose…'

Spencer spent the afternoon in his office, reading *Othello* and making notes for his class the following day.

On Thursday morning Spencer arrived at 9am for his second seminar. There was a new student in the group. Theo Gustafsson dressed in the style that Spencer thought of as Young Fogey. He wore flannel trousers, a burgundy bow-tie and a grey silk shirt. Spencer noticed pearl cuff links with tiny Latin numerals etched onto them in red. He sat separately from the other students.

'So, I trust you've all managed to read *Othello*, because that's the play we're discussing today.'

'Professor Leyton?' It was Chantal, one of the African-American students.

'Er, yes Chantal'

Chantal picked up a piece of paper from her desk and read what was apparently a prepared statement.

> *Following the shocking display of police violence at Wednesday's demonstration we, the students of Pellier University, call on all members of Faculty to support us at next week's protest.*

'Bullshit' muttered Theo Gustafsson.

Chantal stared at him. 'What?'

'Nothing.'

Spencer intervened, 'Okay, Chantal. Look, this is not really the time and place for statements like this. We're here to discuss *Othello*, not local political issues. I mean, maybe if this were a politics class we could talk about it, but it's not really relevant for our purposes.'

'Professor?' it was Dani.

'Yes Dani?'

'You said in the first class that Shakespeare's work was applicable to every human situation.'

'Well, I'm not sure that those were my exact words…'

'So if *Othello* is a play about race and power, then surely we should be talking about the demonstration as part of the discussion.'

'Well, I take your point, but…'

'Professor Murray is going to be addressing the demonstration,' said Chantal.

'Who?'

'Jessica Murray. She's awesome.'

'White lives matter too.'

The entire class turned to look at Theo Gustafsson.

'What did you say?' Chantal's voice was quiet.

'You heard. I'm sick and tired of being told that black lives matter. White lives matter too, and this stupid demonstration just ties up the police when they could be doing something useful, like catching the jerk-offs who stole my car.' He appealed to Spencer, 'I've got a Porsche Boxster. Someone stole it last week and drove it to the other side of town and trashed it. The police know it was some local kids, but they can't pin it on them.'

There was a cold silence.

'Okay,' Spencer tried his 'firm and authoritative' voice, 'I really think we need to return to the matter in hand.'

'Professor Leyton,' it was Dani, 'sadly, the only members of faculty who have so far agreed to join our protest are women. It would send a positive message to have a man on board.'

Theo Gustafsson spoke, 'Maybe men have got more sense than to get mixed up in this bullshit.'

Dani turned on him, 'Why don't you button your lip, frat boy?'

'Er… Theo,' said Spencer, 'we need to retain respectful language if we are to make any progress here.'

'Jesus H. Christ! There you go again! As soon as you don't toe the PC party line you get slapped down. Every damn time.' He stood up. 'I'm going to the bathroom' he said, and started for the door. He stopped and turned, 'Oh, by the way, along with Black History Month, let's have Stop Blaming White People Month.' He left the room.

'Dani,' said Spencer, groping at straws, 'I can't help feeling that as a foreign visitor I should stand apart from all this.

In my experience, you Americans don't take kindly to foreigners telling you how to run the show.'

'London, Bristol, Liverpool,' intoned Chantal, 'all those cities were built on the blood of slaves, so maybe you do have a dog in this fight.'

'Okay, look… I will reflect on the matter and … er… speak to colleagues, and I will consider my position on this.' He paused and stared at a group of sceptical young faces. 'Now please let's talk about *Othello*.'

Every teacher is a performer and every class is a show. Spencer felt that he had walked on stage, tripped over the furniture, and forgotten his lines. He tried to kick-start the discussion. 'Any first thoughts? Themes of the play? Thoughts on the main characters? Er… Mark?'

Mark was wearing a T-shirt with a picture of Andy Warhol on it. He smiled and said nothing.

Shelley put her hand up. She was a tall black woman with braided hair, wearing a Pellier track suit. She wanted to know if Shakespeare had ever met a black person.

'Well, it's hard to say. Certainly there were some black people in London at the time, but it was not multicultural in the way that it is now.'

'So how did he have the nerve to portray a black man if he didn't know anything about them?' asked Shelley.

'Well he didn't know any ancient Romans, but that didn't stop him writing about Julius Caesar. He used his imagination.'

'It doesn't work though, does it?' this time it was Dani.

Spencer took a deep breath, 'William Shakespeare was the son of a glover from Stratford upon Avon. If every single one of his plays had been about the life and adventures of a glover's son from Stratford, I don't think anyone would be reading his plays today. He puts the whole world on the stage. That is what makes him a great writer.'

'Well I can't see what's great about this play', said Chantal, 'Othello is a horrific racial stereotype. He's the lascivious Negro, desperate to get his hands on a white woman. My God haven't we been *there* before?'

Spencer could feel his irritation rise. Were they just trying to get at him?

'Othello,' he began again, 'is the most noble character in the play. And he represents the excluded, the outsider.'

'*Noble*?' said Chantal, 'He's just a sort of exotic idiot. A white audience has their prejudice reaffirmed at the sight of a gullible black man being duped by a clever white man.'

Dani joined the attack, 'And then, good Lord, there's Desdemona. Total white man's fantasy. Submissive, nubile girl who gets punished in the end, because she was sluttish enough to have sex with a black man.'

Spencer stared out of the window for a while. He felt like the singer who has lost his voice, the dancer who has sprained an ankle.

There was now a note of desperation in his voice. 'I'm not saying you're wrong, and of course you have a right to your views, but Shakespeare is without doubt the most performed playwright in the world, and his audience come from all walks of life. I want you to understand just why he is a great writer, and at the moment we are not getting anywhere near that.'

He shuffled his notes on the desk. Theo Gustafsson came back into the room, slamming the door behind him.

Spencer carried on, 'I am sure you'll have a different view of the characters if you try to inhabit them for a moment. Shakespeare's plays were written to be performed, after all. Okay, let's try acting a scene out. Let's get it up on its feet, er… so to speak. Can we clear away some of the chairs and desks and give ourselves some rehearsal space?'

Spencer was pleased to see this operation carried out with a degree of enthusiasm.

'Good. Okay, now first of all we have to cast this scene from Othello. We have more women than men in our group, but that's okay. We can turn a challenge into an opportunity, if you know what I mean. It really is quite commonplace nowadays to have cross-casting in Shakespeare, where women play men, and it can sometimes shed new light on a play, so… Chantal, perhaps you could play Othello and Dani… perhaps you could play Iago.'

'Wait a minute Professor.' It was Theo Gustafsson. 'I think I should play Othello.' This was greeted by a cold silence from the rest of the group.

'Well, look Theo, I think it's probably more appropriate for Chantal to play Othello.'

'Why?'

Spencer was struggling, 'Er… well…'

'You see, Professor, Othello is a man, right? And I am a man. So I should play him.'

'Yeah, but you're white,' said Chantal through clenched teeth.

'So? So what are you saying? That someone's colour is more important than their gender? Is that what you're saying?'

'Well, in this case…' said Chantal.

'Look,' Spencer intervened, 'I think we're getting diverted here…'

'Wait a minute,' said Theo, 'You know that Laurence Oliver?'

'Laurence Oliver? You mean Laurence Olivier?'

'Yeah, him. Well he was a white guy, and I saw a movie of him playing Othello. He wore black make-up.'

The room grew colder.

'You see, Theo, that movie was made in the 1960s, and things have moved on since then.'

'Why the hell do you want to play Othello anyway?' It was Dani.

'Because I want to do some acting.'

'Do you have any experience?'

'Sure do. Back in High School we did *The Sound of Music*. I played a German soldier.'

Chantal started to snigger, 'You mean you played a Nazi? Couldn't they find you a more challenging role?'

Theo was clenching his fists, 'Now wait a fucking minute…'

Spencer watched helplessly as his rehearsal descended into chaos.

CHAPTER THREE

On Friday morning Spencer and Walt were driving in Walt's car. Chuck Berry was on the radio playing 'No Particular Place to Go'. The two men were singing along. They were a few miles outside town when Walt slowed to point out an isolated farmhouse away from the road along a dirt track. 'You see quite a few of these places out here,' said Walt. 'and I sometimes wonder what kind of genetic throwback might live there. I wouldn't drive up uninvited – they can be jealous of their privacy.'

Walt parked at a local beauty spot called Pine Lake. It was a small stretch of water with a forest of pines running up a hill on one side. On this warm cloudless day the water was a clear blue. They strolled for a while.

'Walt, have you had much contact with the local police?'

'They've pulled me over for speeding, but apart from that, no. Have you been talking to Louisa by any chance?'

'Actually, yes.'

Walt laughed, 'Yeah, well she really isn't a fan of Merganserville's finest. I mean, y'know… there are rumours… people have made allegations about them but nothing ever seems to be proved.'

'What kind of allegations?'

'That they treat the black population very differently than the way they treat white people. I've noticed there are hardly any black cops around here. People say that the police have the courts and the judges in their pockets. But how would I know really?' He kicked a stone into the lake.

'Do you have many black friends, Walt?'

'Not since High School, frankly. I mean obviously there are one or two colleagues at Pellier, but not too many, really.'

'Have you ever dated a black woman?'

'No. Why put your head up above the trench?'

They stopped and admired the surface of the lake, shimmering in the sun.

'Are you seeing anyone at the moment then, Walt?'

'No. I'm not even considering offers… if you know what I mean. I just don't know what I want right now. Most women anywhere near my age are trying to find a lifetime partner. The clock is ticking for them as far as children are concerned, and I just don't want that.'

'Are you sure? You see, it went wrong for me in the end, but I would still say that having children is the best thing I ever did… even though I don't see them as much as I would like.'

'Really, it is just not what I want. I'm not even sure that I want a lifetime partner. If I felt that I could spend the rest of my life surrounded by friends of both sexes and had the opportunity for the odd romantic attachment when I wanted it, well… that would be fine, just fine. How about you?'

'I'm lonely, Walt. I have been since my marriage broke up. But also, I just can't imagine who would be right for me now...'

The two men stood in the sun for a few minutes without speaking.

Spencer pointed at a pair of small ducks floating on the water a few metres away.

'What's that bird? The duck with the crest… you see there?'

'That? That's the Hooded Merganser. There's an adult male and an adult female.'

'Is that why this place is called Merganserville?'

'I guess so.'

They watched the two birds travel slowly across the lake.

'They look so content, don't they?' said Spencer

'Well, there's nothing much to bother them. I've never seen anyone out here trying to hunt them.'

'What *do* people hunt?'

'Oh, they shoot at deer, rabbits… and at each other, of course.'

'Do you own a gun?' asked Spencer.

'No. Never owned a gun in my life, but a lot of people here in Georgia do, and will never give them up. Also – and you may find this hard to believe – there is a town not far from here called Kennesaw where it's illegal *not* to own a gun.'

'You have to own a gun *by law*?'

'If you are the head of the household and you can afford one, yes.' Walt chuckled, 'God Bless America.'

They watched the birds on the lake for a while.

'Do they mate for life?' asked Spencer.

'I don't think so. I don't think many ducks do. They tend to be seasonal monogamists.'

'What?'

'The male has to find a new mate every season,' explained Walt.

'*Every* season? My God! – the pressure…'

Walt turned back towards the car, 'Do you like horses, Spencer?'

'Horses? I love them. Why?'

'We can call in on some friends of mine; they have some horses… y'know, I give a lot of money to sick horses.'

Spencer grinned. He knew what was coming.

'Of course,' said Walt, 'I don't know they're sick when I put my money on them.'

They drove back towards town and pulled off into a ranch at the side of the road. The sign at the gate said *Old Man Thompson's Farm.* A woman on a bay quarter horse rode up to greet them. She was about thirty years old and blonde. She wore the standard farmer's outfit of jeans and check shirt.

'Don't tell me,' said Spencer, 'that must be Old Man Thompson.'

Walt laughed, 'I don't think there was ever an Old Man Thompson. Not in living memory, anyway. No, that's Ellie.'

Walt waved a greeting and pulled up at the house. They were met by Ellie's husband, Neil. He was in his mid-thirties, slim, with thinning fair hair. The horses were admired, iced tea was served, and conversation was made in the rocking chairs on the porch. Spencer had a sense that he was playing a character part in a rather clichéd movie about the Old South. Walt and Ellie chatted incessantly about horses, farming and the people they knew locally. Spencer asked polite questions and Neil said very little.

'Will you have time to travel while you're here, Spencer?' Ellie asked, leaning forward and touching him on the arm. She spoke in a classic low Southern drawl.

'Well, I have had some trips with Walt and I plan to visit Palm Springs at Thanksgiving. I have a relative there.'

'Do you play golf?' she asked.

'Er, no…'

'I'm not quite sure what you'll do in Palm Springs then.'

Neil finally put a word in, 'I don't know if you're the type to enjoy the clothing-optional gay resorts…'

'Well he really doesn't look the type, does he Neil?' rebuffed Ellie.

She sipped her tea, 'The one place you have to see while you're in the South is New Orleans. One hundred per cent.'

'We have an apartment there,' Neil chipped in.

'Hey, we're there this weekend,' said Ellie, 'why don't you come visit?'

'New Orleans? Really?' said Spencer.

Walt thought for a moment, 'I have a bunch of stuff to do on Saturday, but we could fly out in the evening. I think we could be with you about ten o'clock.'

'Isn't that a bit late to be arriving?' asked Spencer.

There were guffaws all round. 'Honey, in New Orleans ten in the evening is breakfast time,' said Ellie.

'Okay then,' said Spencer, 'er… thank you.'

As they walked to the car Spencer looked over at the horses. There were four of them, standing close together in a group. As quarter horses they were stockier than the thoroughbreds he had seen at British race courses. The bay horse rested its chin on the withers of the black horse next to him. There was no pressure on a horse to make conversation, thought Spencer.

****

Spencer sent emails to his children, Rosie and Joseph, and attached photos of the campus and his apartment. He thought of sending an email to Sarah, his ex-wife, but could not think of anything to say. He wrote to Jane at his college in London to explain that he had arrived safely and had started teaching.

He spent a few minutes on Facebook. Spencer consciously limited the time he spent on social media: he'd told his friends that he had no desire to be a captive to a screen and he disliked the instant opinion-mill that was Twitter. He had always been a generation behind with new technology. He was still listening to CDs when everyone else was downloading their music. He found CDs convenient, and since most of the music he liked had been recorded on wax cylinders on Mississippi plantations in the 1930s he was not too concerned about which format would provide the best quality.

Late that afternoon Walt picked Spencer up for their night out in Atlanta.

'I'll try to take the scenic route, which means sticking to the back roads for the first part of the trip,' said Walt. 'Also, there's a place I want to show you along the way.'

Spencer gazed out at the scenery. It was one of his first opportunities to see a bit of the countryside. He noticed the iconic red Georgia clay, but with its lush forests much of the land reminded him of Wales.

 He had been in America for less than a week, but already it felt like a lifetime. There had been so much that he had not expected, so many adjustments to be made. People here spoke his language, but much of the time he felt that he was in a culture that was more foreign than anywhere he had been in Europe.

Suddenly, from the trees, a creature the size of a badger streaked across the road. With a flash of brown it shot into the woods.

'What the hell was that?' asked Spencer.

'Groundhog. Or Whistle Pig, as they say round here.'

They drove on through the woods. After a few minutes Walt pulled the car off the road.

They had arrived at a small roadside store. A sign over the door said 'Milt McGrew's Civil War Memorabilia Store'.

On entering, Spencer was struck by a huge display of Confederate flags, Confederate uniforms, Confederate insignia and pictures of Confederate generals. There was a surprising lack of corresponding imagery from the Union side of the conflict.

Everywhere there were glass display cases, all of them thick with dust, showing medals, coins and bullets, always from the Confederate side.

In a glass display case Spencer examined some Civil War weapons. There was a Springfield 1855 rifle, a Burnside carbine and several mid-nineteenth-century revolvers.

The proprietor, Milt McGrew, introduced himself with a thin smile. He was a man in his sixties, with grey shoulder-length hair and an unkempt beard. Like his display cases, he was thick with dust. He wore a revolver on his hip.

'What's that piece you got there, Milt?' asked Walt.

'Oh, this… this isn't Civil War vintage, but it's a historical weapon okay.' He pulled it from its holster, 'This is a 1917 Colt.'

'Does it work?' asked Spencer.

Milt replied slowly, as if addressing a charmingly naïve young child. 'Well, I wouldn't be carrying it if it didn't work, now, would I?'

Spencer looked at a huge portrait of Stonewall Jackson and moved on to another display. The items here seemed later than the Civil War material. They included some daggers emblazoned with the letters KKK.

He walked back to a separate room at the back of the store. There a sign above the door reading 'No Dogs, No Negroes, No Mexicans'. It had been amended to read 'Dogs okay'. Spencer walked through the door. Directly in front of him was a life-size mannequin in a full Ku Klux Klan uniform. The mannequin was holding a noose. Disgust rising within him, Spencer turned on his heel.

'I think it's probably time to go,' he said to Walt.

Seated in the car, Walt pulled out a coin.

'What's that?'

'This is a Confederate half-dollar coin,' said Walt.

'Where did you get that?'

'In the store.'

'I didn't notice you buy it.'

'I didn't buy it.' Walt chuckled and slipped it back into his pocket. 'Do you think I'd give money to that bastard?'

They drove on. Spencer lowered the window and lit a cigarette.

Walt grunted at him, 'Nobody does that any more y'know.'

'Well then, I must be nobody.'

Walt powered the car back onto the freeway. It was sunset when they arrived at their destination – a one-storey building on the main drag, just north of downtown Atlanta. A neon sign proclaimed, 'The Purple Pussycat Strip Club'. Whatever Spencer had been expecting it was not this.

Walt pulled up outside the building.

'You can tell Louisa that you came here to find out more about women's issues, hahaha. Ever been to one of these places before?'

'Once, when I was about twenty, in Soho. I was with a bunch of lads and we were all pretty drunk. I don't remember too much about it.'

At least the music isn't too loud, thought Spencer as they went in. The room was larger than he had anticipated from the outside, dimly-lit, apart from the central area which was dominated by a circular stage with a pole going up to the ceiling. There were tables and plush upholstered chairs grouped around the stage, and at the side of the room was a row of semi-private booths. Several of these were in use, with an almost-naked woman writhing around on a seated customer. There were other women in lingerie or fetish-wear moving around the room approaching individual men to offer private dances.

The two men sat at the bar.

'So I bet you don't feel like you're in a minority now, eh Spencer?' said Walt.

Spencer smiled. 'I'm not sure what to feel. To be honest with you, I find it a bit strange.'

'Look, you get your money's worth in this place. It's $10 for a lap dance, then there's a VIP room at the back which costs a little more, but you can get the girls to go a little further, if you know what I mean. If you're short of cash I can lend you some, no problem.'

Walt looked at an auburn-haired woman in a basque and suspenders who was talking to customers on the other side of the room.

'There she is – my favourite. See you in a little while.'

Walt crossed the room and the woman greeted him like an old friend. They retired to one of the booths.

Spencer ordered a beer and looked around him. He was reminded of the first time he went to a casino. There was a tension in the air, a heat, a sense of expectation – but expectation of what, exactly?

There were perhaps fifty customers, all of them men and all of them white. They seemed to be mostly around his age. The dancers, of course, were considerably younger. There was something about seeing all this female flesh on sale (or at least for rent) that was making him feel a little queasy. Spencer had long felt that human beings play roles every moment of their lives. A man may begin his day as a father, then spend some time in the role of a commuter, then as a work-colleague, then as a friend, finally ending his day in the role of a husband. There is no element of deception about any of this and we move from one guise to another without effort. Here, as a punter in a strip club, Spencer felt woefully miscast.

'Alright now,' the DJ's voice boomed out, 'next on stage we have one of our most popular girls – let's hear it for Sherree!'

The music started – 'Legs' by ZZ Top – and a tall, slender young woman with waist-length dark hair came out onto the stage. She was wearing a lacy bra, a G-string and high-heeled, thigh-length boots. The bra came off fairly soon and Spencer realised that he could never be attracted to a woman with breast implants. Sherree spent the next few minutes coiling herself around the pole, displaying impressive gymnastic abilities. Spencer was starting to feel bored.

Sherree's dance finished to desultory applause and Spencer looked around at the customers. Did they come here every week? Did they have wives and children at home? Was this just a descendant of the American tradition of Burlesque?

The DJ announced 'Samantha – the girl in the mask' and Cyndi Lauper's 'Time After Time' played over the speakers. Suddenly Spencer began to take an interest. Samantha wore a silver wig and a highwayman's mask covering her eyes, along with a basque, suspenders, a G-string and heels. There was something enticing about the way she moved and when she took off the basque Spencer was reassured that her breasts were natural. He thought he had never seen a more beautiful body, and there was something very erotic about the mask. On her knees, then on all fours, she began to pout and wriggle, teasing the men sitting in the front row. She enacted various male fantasies, including a few that Spencer had never imagined. As an academic in the field of drama he should have been considering it all in terms of performance versus performativity and the construction of gender. But he wasn't. He moved from the bar and took a seat a little distance from the stage. He let his gaze drift from her breasts to her face.

It was Dani. Even with the mask, he was absolutely sure. It was his student Dani.

It was crucial that she did not see him. Slowly, as inconspicuously as possible, he crept from his seat and moved to the back of the room. He gulped his drink. His pulse was racing. Had she seen him?

Walt reappeared, 'Money well spent,' he said with a grin. 'Are you gonna have a private dance? Any of the girls catch your eye?'

'Look, Walt,' began Spencer, 'I really appreciate you taking me out like this but er…, well…this place just isn't me, I'm afraid…'

Walt laughed and slapped him on the shoulder, 'Goddammit you're not gay after all, are you Spencer my man?'

'No, really I'm not, but this place… I just don't feel very comfortable. Could we maybe go and get something to eat?'

'Well you know you're getting old when you'd rather eat than look at gorgeous semi-naked women, but actually I am hungry, so, yeah, let's go. I know a great place a couple of blocks away.'

At Spencer's insistence they made the three-minute journey on foot. Walt was baffled as to why they did not take the car. As they walked into the Rawhide Steak

House, Walt said with a wink, 'The food's great here and so is the service.'

Predictably, every one of the waitresses was young and attractive, and wearing a very short skirt. 'See what I mean?' said Walt, grinning broadly.

The two men were shown to a table.

'Walt, look,' Spencer hesitated, 'I really like you and you've been very kind to me, and I mean I like a pretty girl as much as the next man but…'

'But can I stop waving my dick in your face?'

'Well, I don't know that I would have put it quite that way…'

Walt burst out laughing and gave a cod imitation of Spencer's English accent, 'Oh my dear fellow if you wouldn't mind frightfully not waving your male member in the vicinity of my visage hahaha.' For once, Walt looked as though he were about to discuss something seriously, 'Spencer, I've worked with British men before and I really do think there is a cultural difference. Did it occur to you that I am the product of a puritan culture? Over the last few years there have been so many changes that it does start to feel like there's a new Puritanism alive and well. And yes, some of us do get defensive about it. I bite my tongue every day because I'm worried that something I say might be misinterpreted, but honestly, Spencer, I am not a raving sexist. My parents' marriage was a partnership of equals and I learnt from my father how to treat women with respect. But please do allow me to let my hair down occasionally, because it's all just fantasy.'

Spencer smiled and nodded, 'That's fine with me Walt, and anyway who am I to tell you how to behave?'

Walt nodded and glanced at the menu, 'I suppose you drink wine, don't you?'

'Well, you know, sometimes.'

'I just don't see the point.'

'What?'

'Beer is refreshing, cocktails make the world a better place. Wine? Why bother?'

'I'll tell Baron Rothschild next time I see him,' grunted Spencer.

'Hello, I'm Sylvia and I'm your server this evening,' said the young blonde woman who had just arrived at the table. 'Can I take your drink order?'

'Brooklyn East for me,' said Walt

'Brooklyn East?' said Spencer, 'What's that?'

'It's an IPA, pretty strong.'

'Fine, I'll have that too. Look, Walt, what would you recommend to eat?'

'You have to have the rump steak – comes with fries and a side salad.'

Spencer nodded.

'How do y'all want them done?' asked Sylvia.

'Rare as you can cook it,' said Walt.

'Well done,' said Spencer.

'He's English – he really means well done, so tell them to throw it on the grill for two-and-a-half hours, but I really want it rare so pull its horns off, wipe its ass and send it in here. And I'll have French on the salad.'

'Dressing on the salad?' Sylvia asked Spencer, 'We have French, Italian, Ranch, Thousand Island, Blue Cheese, Honey Mustard…'

'No dressing at all, thanks.'

For a moment two Americans looked at him aghast.

The drinks arrived and Walt continued his analysis of sexual politics.

'Look Spencer let me tell you this: I don't like it when people create differences that aren't there. Do you remember those books with titles like *Men are from Mars and Women are from the Planet Zog*? Well I just don't get it. We're all the same species, aren't we?'

'But some men genuinely don't understand why they can't flirt with women in the office without ending up on the Sex Offenders list,' said Spencer.

'Well I think they protest too much as that bald guy from Stratford put it. We reproduce as a species by flirting, but flirting is not sexual harassment and I think the line is quite clear. It's just common sense. The problem, of course, is when large amounts of alcohol are involved. We have had so many cases where our students' judgement is clouded by alcohol, and they just don't read the signs. But when a male student ignores the word No... well, that's not about being a man, that's about being an asshole, and there have to be consequences. And this has been pointed out on our campus so often that the boys really should have got the message by now.'

'What about affairs between members of staff? Does that go on much?'

'Well, you're a fast mover aren't you? You've spotted someone you like already?'

'No, no...'

'I think you'll find that the office romance is alive and well.'

'Do you ever hear of teachers dating students? I mean, I know it's against the rules, but does it ever happen?'

'I've never heard of it happening here and, goddammit, I hope I never will. That would be totally unacceptable to me.'

When the steaks arrived they were each the size of the average double mattress.

Spencer's steak was quite well done enough. Walt's steak was so rare it was still moving.

'Walt, you know that place you took me to today – that Confederate store?'

'Milt McGrew's – yep.'

'Back home, that place would have been closed down. It would be illegal under the Race Relations Act.'

'Yeah, well… freedom of speech is enshrined in the Constitution.'

'Freedom to incite racial hatred?'

'I think the way it's seen here… it's a question of context.' Walt chewed on his steak, 'You wouldn't be allowed to hand out anti-Semitic leaflets outside a synagogue, for example, but it's okay to sell that kind of thing in your own store. I guess that's the way they look at it here.'

'But you personally… do you think that's right?'

Walt smiled, 'I'm an academic. I just have to present different points of view. I don't have to have an opinion myself.'

****

Spencer was in the passenger seat and Walt was driving to the airport. He was smoking a briar pipe. This surprised Spencer.

'It's a Kapp and Peterson, don't you know,' said Walt, brandishing the pipe.

There was a yapping sound behind Spencer. He turned, and was shocked to see a small dog on the back seat. It was chewing furiously at what seemed to be a human femur.

'Is this your dog?'

'Yep,' said Walt, 'He's coming on the plane with us. He's called Simba.'

'Can you do that? I mean, does he have to have his own seat?' Spencer turned back to Walt, who had ditched the pipe and was wearing a red turban.

'Don't worry about it. It's absolutely nothing to worry about.' Walt burst into uncontrollable laughter.

'It's nearly six o'clock,' snarled Spencer, 'We're going to miss the plane…'

Walt's manic laughter continued. A snake had crawled into the car and was attacking the dog. Walt took both hands off the wheel and belaboured the snake with a machete. The car careered off the road and into a ditch. With the snake writhing in its death throes, Pope John XXIII stepped into the car and began to administer the Last Rites.

'Are you speaking *ex cathedra?*' barked the dog. The Pope looked remorseful and nibbled the ears of a camel. A quarter horse climbed through the window, playing the harmonica and singing. 'I woke up this morning,' sang the horse. On the hood of the car Dani, scantily dressed, was dancing to the music.

'The lunatics have taken over the asylum!' yelled Walt, the machete spinning in his hands. Screaming for help, Spencer tried to escape, but the doors were locked.

'Are you all right?' It was Walt's voice. He was no longer wearing a turban. 'You were making some really weird noises.'

Spencer was in an aeroplane seat, wet with perspiration. 'Oh… bad dream… '

His bad dream had been hardly surprising. He had worked himself into a frenzy of stress in his apartment, waiting for Walt, who was late to pick him up.

'I don't think we're going to make it,' Spencer had said, piling into the car, 'we're supposed to check in two hours before the flight.'

Walt snorted, 'That's just a bunch of 9/11 bullshit. I once got to the airport twenty minutes before the flight and managed to get on board.' He stamped on the accelerator. Tentacles of stress began to crawl up Spencer's spine. Walt drove at his usual manic speed all the way to the airport. Hartsfield-Jackson is the world's busiest airport and Walt struggled to find a parking space. The tentacles of stress were by now grasping Spencer by the throat. They made the flight moments before the gate closed.

'You see,' said Walt, 'I told you there wouldn't be a problem.'

The plane came into Louis Armstrong airport a few minutes ahead of schedule and Neil picked them up in a BMW. It was dark when they reached the apartment that Neil and Ellie kept on the edge of the French Quarter. With its shuttered windows and wrought iron balconies the house, and indeed the neighbourhood, were very different from anything Spencer had yet seen in America. The area seemed to date from the mid-nineteenth century, and the apartment, with its high ceilings and antique furniture, seemed to evoke a time long gone by.

Spencer and Walt dropped their bags in the room they were to share for their stay.

'Who's coming out for a drink?' asked Neil, grinning broadly.

'Yes, I'm up for it,' said Spencer.

'Actually, I'm a little tired,' said Walt, 'I guess I'll stay here for a while.'

'I'll keep you company,' said Ellie. She turned to the other two men, 'We'll catch up with you later.'

Spencer was, to say the least, surprised.

CHAPTER FOUR

It was a fine night in New Orleans and the streets were teeming with people. Spencer thought they were mostly tourists rather than locals. There was a wide range of ages and types – the common denominator being that they were all totally rat-arsed. Neil dragged Spencer into a bar called Le Maison de New Orleans. No prizes for originality, thought Spencer. It was a mostly older crowd, with a jazz band playing in the corner. Neil elbowed his way to the bar, shouting over his shoulder at Spencer, 'You gotta have a Mint Julep. This place does the best in town.'

At the bar, Spencer found himself standing next to a man wearing a baseball cap with the slogan 'Make America Weird Again'. As usual, Spencer's accent caused comment. A man in a Lakers T-shirt grabbed him, 'Hey, you from England, right?'

Spencer nodded assent.

'England's in London, right?'

'That's right.'

'My cousin Dave lives in London. Do you know him? He lives on the North Side.'

'Ah,' said Spencer apologetically, 'I'm afraid not. You see, I live on the South Side, and I haven't got around to applying for a permit to cross the river.'

A young woman pushed her face into his, 'Did you know Princess Diana?'

'Yeah, but not too well, y'know. Lunch, never dinner.'

A short, bearded man sidled up.

'Is it right that in your National Health System you have to go before a panel when you get to the age of seventy, and if you can't pass the fitness test they execute you?'

'That's right,' said Spencer, 'and we cook the body parts and feed them to our servants.'

The man thought for a while and said, 'Y'know, that's not such a bad idea.'

The mint julep was followed by another and then they were out and heading along Bourbon Street. Even with a couple of drinks inside him, Spencer was starting to wonder if this nocturnal excursion with Neil would prove to be a bad idea.

Human sexuality can be seen as a spectrum. At one end are people who identify as exclusively straight, at the other are those who identify as exclusively gay – with many diversions and off-shoots along the way. Some of us move about on this spectrum during a lifetime, or even during the course of a week. Spencer had once known a man called Sam who was heterosexual in Liverpool and homosexual in Manchester. He spent the working week with his girlfriend in Liverpool and then on Friday evening would drive off to be with his boyfriend in

Manchester. No one was exactly sure where the transition from straight to gay took place. Perhaps it was at the Burtonwood services on the M62.

In New Orleans, this spectrum is represented by Bourbon Street. The south-west end, by Canal Street, teems with strip clubs and stag parties, the north-east end beyond Philip Street is studded with gay bars and drag acts. Spencer and Neil crawled along Bourbon Street, stopping at every bar. Nearly every place they entered had some sort of live music, and the bands seemed to get louder as the night went on. Even outside the bars there were street musicians howling their way through the blues. Spencer found himself in shouted conversations with total strangers. There was an attempt at dancing with a woman from Philadelphia. He was cracking jokes and telling stories to bemused Americans. The journey lasted most of the night, and through it all the alcohol flowed, with the musky smell of marijuana on every corner. Despite the general level of intoxication the atmosphere was edgy, but not threatening. Certainly, Spencer had seen far worse in Birmingham on a Friday night.

Long after midnight, near Philip Street, Neil propelled a by now drunk Spencer into a bar festooned with rainbow flags. 'RuPaul's Drag Race' was showing on a huge screen and the customers were watching with great enthusiasm, often shouting and cheering as if they were at a sports event. Several of the crowd greeted Neil, and he was soon in close conversation with a group of younger men. Spencer, who dressed for anonymity rather than display, felt a little out of place – but he was really too far gone to care. The barman put a shot-glass in front of Spencer and filled it with bourbon. 'I didn't order this…' Spencer said. The barman nodded at Neil, who was over the other side of the room 'He sent it over.'

Eventually, in the small hours of the morning, Spencer found himself in a bar near the corner of Bourbon Street and Barracks Street, hunched over a table staring at a beer he did not want. At the next table, a lesbian couple, surrounded by their rowdy friends, were celebrating an anniversary. On a tiny stage in front of him Anna Condom (billed as 'New Orleans Best Drag Queen') was strumming a guitar and crooning 'If I Could Turn Back Time'. Neil had disappeared long ago.

Anna Condom finished the song and asked for any requests. A few suggestions were grunted drunkenly from around the room. She looked straight at Spencer.

'How about you? Do you have a request, other than for a cab, given the state you're in – which happens to be Louisiana.'

'Do you know how to sing the blues?' Spencer slurred back.

Anna played an arpeggio and thought for a moment, then launched into song,

'I'm going down to St. James Infirmary/To see my baby there…'

She sang it perfectly, the story of grief and loss silencing the drunken crowd. Spencer started to cry. Anna finished the set, thanked the audience and sat down at the table with him.

'Are you alright, honey?'

Spencer blew his nose, 'Yes, yes, I'm fine, really. I'm just drunk, y'know… and that song… as you get older… as you get older you lose things, don't you? Things are taken from you.'

'Sure, but you gain a few things too. You get to know yourself a little better, don't you? Well, I did. You're from England?'

'Yes. Sorry… I don't know your cousin Ambrose in Sheffield.'

Anna laughed out loud, 'I had all that when I first arrived. I grew up in a place called Market Harborough. I came here thirty years ago.'

'Market Harborough…? We were neighbours. I'm from Kettering. You don't sound…'

'I ditched the accent as soon as I could. Then I changed my name, changed the way I look, changed everything… I reinvented myself, and I've never been back to Market Harborough.' She squeezed his hand, 'I've got to go. Take care of yourself, sweetheart.'

The door was unlocked, and Spencer let himself in. Walt's bed was empty. Neil was nowhere to be seen. Spencer collapsed on the sofa in the living room and immediately fell asleep. He was woken at dawn by the sounds of passion from Ellie and Neil's bedroom. The sounds were not being made by Ellie and Neil but by Ellie and Walt.

Spencer went to bed.

****

Spencer, Walt, Ellie and Neil were having lunch, if lunch is the word for a meal that starts at four in the afternoon when you've only just got out of bed.

They sat on the terrace of a small restaurant near the apartment. Dark glasses hid Spencer's bloodshot eyes. And his thoughts. Nothing was said of the events of the night before. Did Neil know about Walt and Ellie? How long had that been going on? Where had Neil ended up the night before and with whom? Spencer stared at the three of them, amazed at how such duplicity could be sustained with such apparent ease. Assuming that it was duplicity. When he came back to the conversation the topic had moved to the removal of Confederate statues.

'Why are they always pickin' on us?' said Ellie, a whine in her voice, 'Why can't they just stay up north and leave us alone?'

Behind his shades, Spencer stared at her. Was there still so much resentment against the Yankee nation? Why did the Civil War still loom so large in the American psyche, or at least that part of it that resided in the South? It had been over for 150 years – why not let it go?

Spencer's hosts insisted that he should finish lunch with a beignet. This New Orleans speciality turned out to be a cardiac-arresting piece of fried dough covered in powdered sugar. Spencer finished this treat with some difficulty.

'Do you mind if I take a walk?' he smiled, 'I need to work this off. I've got my phone – can we catch up later?'

He walked along the Riverfront, then sat on a bench, lit a cigarette and watched a cruise ship gliding through the muddy water of the Mississippi. Spencer had long felt that the defining moment for the British was Dunkirk, and with it the idea that the nation had stood together through the Second World War, the risks and privations falling equally on Prince and Pauper. This was clearly a myth; there were no ration books at the Savoy. Then, of course, came the Dad's Army myth: Spencer had a good idea that the impetus for that people's militia came not from suburban Tory bank managers but from the men of the Left who had returned from fighting in Spain. Whatever the historical facts, the British were succoured by their shared view of their history. They were happy to exist with a kind of fudge of Churchill, Vera Lynn and the plucky British Tommy as the vanquishers of the Third Reich. The Americans were apparently too late and surplus to requirements. What happened at Stalingrad was, of course, irrelevant.

It was different in the USA. Black vs White, South vs North, Red states vs Blue states. The War against Slavery or the War of Northern Aggression: take your pick. The nation was divided by two versions of history and two widely different aspirations for the future. That had just not been the case in Britain.

Until Brexit.

Spencer walked to the bottom of Canal Street and found himself opposite Harrah's casino. It was vast: a cathedral of gambling. He crossed the street and walked through the door. He had not been in a casino for well over two years. He looked about him at the row upon row of slot machines. Even in the late afternoon it was busy. He knew that for many of the people there this represented a little harmless fun, a few minutes of escapism. For him, it was different. For him, it had been a compulsion, and his gambling life had been sustained by an ever-growing spiral of lies. For him, the slots, the screens, the lights, the noise – they all sat on a platform of falsehood. He turned and left.

It was, of course, Walt's idea that their second evening in New Orleans should be spent watching Pelvis Lee 'New Orleans Best Elvis Impersonator'. Ellie was keen to go, Spencer decided to tag along and Neil went off on his own somewhere.

Louisiana's answer to the King had opted for the seventies Vegas version in rhinestone jumpsuit. His impersonation of the older Elvis was unintentionally accurate: he was very overweight and looked as though he could be addicted to opiates. However, with a strong voice and a decent four-piece band he put on a good show. For Spencer it was an enjoyable piece of kitsch, despite the awkwardness he felt with Walt and Ellie.

'This one's a classic,' smiled Walt, as The King went into 'You Ain't Nothin' but a Hound Dog'.

'Actually I prefer Ma Rainey's version,' said Spencer.

'But you do like Elvis?' asked Walt.

'Oh yes, I do.'

'You should go to Graceland while you're in the States,' said Ellie.

'Graceland?' said Spencer. 'Is that where Michael Jackson lived?'

'Hahaha! No you idiot; it's where Elvis lived.'

'Well… Michael Jackson and Elvis Presley – pretty much the same.'

Walt thought for a moment.

'Elvis was white. Michael Jackson was… kinda orange, eventually. Elvis liked teenage girls. Michael Jackson liked pre-pubescent boys. Elvis liked sandwiches made of peanut butter, bananas and bacon. Michael Jackson probably never ate anything.'

'Does it put you off?'

'What?'

'There's a sleazy side to Elvis and I just wonder if it stops you listening to the music.'

'Well, clearly it doesn't. Chuck Berry wasn't exactly a pussycat, but I love his music. Where do you draw the line? Wagner was a Nazi, wasn't he?'

'I think for most people today the Michael Jackson thing steps over a line,' said Spencer. 'Paedophilia is our biggest taboo and I totally get that.'

'A hundred and fifty years ago children were commodities,' said Walt. 'You could do what you liked with them. But two consenting men could not have sex together.'

'Thank God times change.'

'So do you want to go to Graceland?'

'Well… I'm not that bothered, really.'

'So if you don't want to see Elvis' house, then maybe you'd like to see his wart.'

'His *what*?'

'His wart. There's a museum of Elvis memorabilia in Georgia. It's in a little place called Cornelia, and they have a wart on display. It's genuine. A doctor cut it from his wrist just before he went into the army.'

'And they have it on display like a saint's relic – like the arm of St Valerie?'

'Exactly like that. Do you want to go? We could go straight from the airport.'

'Are you serious?'

'Serious as a heart attack.'

Spencer laughed. 'Yes, okay. Why not.'

Spencer and Walt took an early flight on Monday morning. Walt was dozing. Spencer was looking out of the window. He was still waiting for Walt to make some sort of comment on what had occurred.

Walt opened his eyes and turned, 'So what did you make of New Orleans?'

'Well… it's quite a place, isn't it? It's really different.'

'Sure is.'

'How about you, Walt? Did you have a good time?'

'Sure did.'

Walt closed his eyes. Spencer looked out of the window.

******

The maples and oaks were starting to take on their autumn colours as they drove out from the airport towards

Cornelia. Spencer fiddled with the radio. Every station seemed to be playing country music or praising the Lord.

'Can't you get any black music round here? This is supposed to be the home of the blues.'

I'm sure you can find some blues if you try.'

Spencer turned the dial, working his way through avaricious evangelists fundraising through prayer power, through commercials by tax accountants who depicted the IRS as, at best, a branch of organised crime and at worst the spawn of Satan himself, through the fog of working-class white triumphalism that was country music.

'Good grief,' said Spencer eventually, 'what is it with these people?'

'What are you talking about?

'Country music. It seems to be all about my dawg, my girl, and my gun.'

'So? There are worse things to care about. Anyway, you can't tell me that the blues is any more progressive.'

'Oh come on Walt… the blues is a great art form.'

'I'd say it was as formulaic as country music. With the blues a guy tells you that he's just woken up in the morning and feels miserable about it – and then he tells you again. And then he tells you that he's not going to do anything to make himself feel better because he's got the blues and he's stuck with them.'

'There's much more to it than that.'

'Look, Spencer, as a limey you can't be expected to understand this, but country music and the blues are just two sides of the coin. They both try to show a day in the life of an American working man – or woman, sometimes. Country represents white traditions and the blues represents black ones. Simple as that. And, as it happens, there are quite a few black country singers nowadays.'

'So I take it you vote Republican?'

'Why do you assume that? Country music has changed … anyway,' Walt chuckled, 'If you don't like Hank Williams you can kiss my ass.'

Spencer laughed and turned back to the radio dial. He found some jazz and decided that would have to do.

They arrived in Cornelia and stopped for lunch. Their waitress seemed sincerely interested in whether or not they were having a nice day. This must be southern hospitality, thought Spencer. Walt chose catfish and grits. Spencer didn't.

They came to the Cornelia Elvis Presley Museum. Objectively, thought Spencer, creating a shrine to Elvis Presley in Cornelia, Georgia is no more peculiar than twisting Shakespeare's birthplace into the commercial monstrosity that is Stratford-upon-Avon. So why did it seem so weird? Perhaps it was the scale of it, with over thirty thousand items. Most of those items were simply photos of The King from birth to untimely death, but there were also numerous Presley-themed dolls, cups, plates, playing cards, scarves, towels and curios with – at the centre of it all – The Wart. The provenance of the wart was beyond doubt. The museum's owner had bought it from the very doctor who sheared it from the Presley wrist. It sat in a tube of formaldehyde on a shrine of red velvet for the faithful to revere.

The museum coffee shop boasted the chance to '*Sample Elvis' favourite dishes – come in and eat like The King!*' Spencer could feel his arteries hardening as he went in. There were, of course, the legendary peanut butter and bacon cheeseburgers, but Spencer was intrigued by Elvis' favourite dessert – something called a Moon Pie. This turned out to be a lunar-shaped cake-and-marshmallow confection, to be washed down with RC cola. Walt and Spencer stuck to coffee.

'Isn't this the weirdest museum you've ever seen?' asked Walt.

'Well, it's up there. Back home we have a lawnmower museum. It's in a place called Southport.'

'*Lawnmowers*? Jesus.' Walt took a sip of coffee, 'Of course, New Orleans has a Museum of Death.'

'Well, some would say that the whole of Southport is a Museum of Death.'

They paid the bill, and Spencer said he was going to the gents.

'Be careful. He might be in there. With Lenny Bruce in the next cubicle.'

Spencer chuckled, 'On the face of it, a Jew like Lenny Bruce and a hillbilly like Elvis – well, they wouldn't seem to have much in common.'

'Except that their biographies were both written by Albert Goldman.'

'And they both finished up grossly overweight, whacked on drugs and dying on the toilet.'

The sun had gone down on an autumn North Georgia day when a sign told them they had twenty-five miles till they reached Merganserville.

'So how did it all start for you?' asked Spencer.

'How did what all start? Bird-watching? Alcoholism? An un-healthy interest in female goats?'

'Teaching in a university.'

'Oh, that…' Walt took a deep breath. 'I'm from Kentucky, and my dad was a veterinarian; we were pretty comfortable financially. They sent me off to study in New York. I majored in drama and spent most of my time seeing plays, so I thought I would be an actor. I graduated, and spent two years in New York being an actor, or not being an actor most of the time. I mean I went to castings, but I just didn't get the jobs. I spent a few weeks in a repertory theatre in Connecticut, I did a couple of shows off-off-off Broadway, but the rest of the time I made a living driving a van around Brooklyn.'

'It sounds like a tough kind of life.'

'I loved it. Just loved it. I had no money, but I didn't care. I knew lots of people in the same situation and it was just… exciting. I mean now… I know I have a pay check coming at the end of the month, but it's all a bit too predictable for me.'

'So what happened then?'

'I got it into my head that I needed more qualifications. I took a Masters in acting at UCLA. I am not quite sure how I thought that would help.'

'But it's what the kids all do now,' Spencer interjected. 'They get their bachelor's degree, and then they see that there are very few openings in their chosen field, so they do a Masters and then a PhD, and then they throw in an MBA for good measure and they're still waiting for openings in their chosen field. They may as well wait for the Second Coming.'

'So what would you advise them to do?'

'I don't know. Get a job in the post room and work your way up. Just don't be an eternal student. Sorry, Walt, you said you were at UCLA?'

'I did my Master's, which was great, but then I was no nearer getting a job when I finished. I was just an unemployed actor in LA rather than New York.' Walt paused, 'And that, I'm afraid, was when things went a little bit wrong for me.'

They drove in silence for a couple of minutes.

'Do you want to tell me about it?'

'Yeah, sure… I mean I don't tell many people, but I don't mind. I started getting into drugs, and particularly cocaine. It developed, the way those things do… and… Oh my God, I don't believe it!'

Looming up at the side of the road was a large clapperboard building. In neon lights above the door was the message 'The BRANDING IRON Roadhouse'. The neon of the letter I in Iron had burnt out, so the sign read BRANDING RON. Underneath came the message 'Tonite: comedian Dave Whittier (hold your sides before they split!). Cold beer. Ribs.'

Walt pulled the car into the car park. A sign on the door told them that guns were prohibited. They walked into a crowded bar. Spencer realised that he was almost the only man in the room not wearing a baseball cap or a cowboy hat.

Dave Whittier, in Stetson and cowboy boots, was onstage, telling a story about an old lady pulled over by a cop.

'Jesus,' Walt muttered to Spencer, 'This one is so old you could carbon-date it.'

'A police officer stopped a little old lady driving a tad over the speed limit. One of the first questions he asked her after the obligatory 'Do you know why I pulled you over?' and 'May I see your license and proof of insurance?' was if she had any firearms in her vehicle. Her reply was that, yes, she had a .357 magnum in her bag. He was taken aback… I mean, she was a little old lady, right? So he asked her if she had any more firearms in the

vehicle.' It was at this point that Spencer realised there were people in the audience who were mouthing the words along with Dave Whittier as if they were joining in with a familiar and well-loved song. *'She sighed and told him that she had a little 9mm M&P Shield in the glove box. His eyes got big, and then he just had to ask one more time. Is that all the firearms in your vehicle? She kind of slumped down and sighed even bigger than before as she told him she had a 12-gauge pump action shotgun in the trunk. That's when he asked his final question on the subject. "Dang lady, what in the world are you afraid of anyways?"*

At that she sat up and looked him dead in the eye and said, "Not a DAMN thing."'

The punchline was greeted by considerable laughter and applause.

Dave Whittier then asked the audience, 'Who is your ideal woman?'

A few names were shouted from the audience. Spencer was familiar with the name Jessica Alba. Someone at the back of the room shouted 'Beyoncé'. Obscenities were shouted back at him.

'I think maybe someone's come to the wrong place,' observed Whittier, 'There's a few places down in Union City might suit you better. The ones that serve soul food.'

Spencer was starting to feel uncomfortable.

'Well, since you ask,' said Whittier, 'I guess my ideal woman fucks till three in the morning and then turns into a pizza.' This was greeted by guffaws throughout the room. Spencer realised that he had heard the joke some twenty years earlier, told by a woman about her idea of the ideal man. He had laughed at the time, so why did inverting the joke make him feel uneasy?

Spencer noticed a group of men at a nearby table. One of them, a weasel-like character in a baseball cap with the yellow John Deere logo, was showing his knife to the others. It was a vicious looking instrument with a serrated edge.

'So they allow knives, but not guns?' muttered Spencer.

Walt shrugged, 'It's a farming area and farmers have knives as part of their job.'

Dave Whittier left the stage, to be replaced by a five-piece band called Wayne Withers and His Prairie Dogs. They kicked off with some classics of country music, starting with 'Don't the girls look prettier at closing time?' by Mickey Gilley, followed by 'I've never gone to bed with an ugly woman but I sure woke up with a few', by Bobby Bare, before swooping into 'I found Jesus on the jailhouse floor', by George Strait, which featured a blistering solo from Wayne Withers on telecaster.

When the band took a break, Walt suggested they make their way back home.

A man at the door seemed to be taking an interest in them. He was in his fifties, with a scrubby grey beard. He wore a T-shirt emblazoned with the confederate flag. He was holding a half-empty beer bottle and swaying a little.

'Are you boys from up north?'

'Nope. He's from England and I'm from Louisville.'

'Well, Louisville is up north as far as I'm concerned. As for England – I ain't too sure where that is.'

'But we live in Merganserville right now,' supplied Spencer helpfully.

'Merganserville? Jesus Christ! Y'all been having a whole lot of trouble with the niggers in Merganserville! Riots, and God knows what. Still, we aim to nip that in the bud. Oh yessir.' He pulled his forefinger across his throat in a cutting gesture and laughed.

Walt looked at Spencer, 'Well, I guess we should be getting on our way.'

The man grabbed Spencer by the arm. 'Only thing you need to understand if you want to get on with us folks is this: 'Scratch a Nigger and you've got a Jew.' That's all you need to know.'

Spencer stared at him, 'What on earth…?'

'Where do you think those blacks get the money to buy all those guns and bombs? Who do y'all think is behind all this anyways? Yessir. Welcome to the good ol' Jew SA' He laughed. 'You don't need to worry, 'cuz we're gonna smoke those Jews out, hahaha, smoke 'em out. Just like Hitler did – smoke 'em out hahaha.'

'We'd really better go,' said Walt, dragging Spencer out into the cool night air.

'We got Parnell with us now and he sure knows how to smoke 'em out. Parnell Prince for President hahaha.'

'What is he talking about?' asked Spencer.

'Let's just get in the car and get going.'

The man stumbled after them. He came to a halt and took a swig of beer. From his lips erupted a high-pitched scream, a 'YipYipYip' that sounded almost like a hunting horn.

'What the fuck?'

'Get in the car.'

Walt pulled the car back onto the highway and they drove for a while in silence.

'Er… Walt… did we just meet the local nutter or does he represent something?'

'Oh yes he represents something alright. You know in Sicily they don't talk about the Mafia? Here we don't talk about the Klan. It doesn't mean it doesn't exist.'

'What the hell was that screaming noise?'

'It's the Rebel Yell. It's the cry the confederate troops made when they went into battle. It was meant to intimidate the enemy, just like a Scottish regiment with the bagpipes.'

'Well it intimidated me.' Spencer thought for a moment, 'But all that stuff about the Jews?'

'So he's a Nazi. He probably thinks Treblinka was a dry-cleaning service.'

'Is it true that Jews came down from the north to help black people?'

'During the Civil Rights struggle? Yes, they did. And earlier too. They put themselves on the line for black people.'

'Why the hell did they do that? Didn't they have enough problems themselves, already?'

Walt drove for a minute or so and then spoke, 'Spencer, did you never read what Pastor Niemöller said?'

'Oh, yeah… 'First they came for the socialists… '

'And I did not speak out because I was not a socialist. And in the end there was no one left to speak out. So check your privilege, Spencer.'

'Well, I'm just glad I am not in this fight. Were you scared in there? I can tell you that I was.'

'Look, I know how to handle myself. I learnt that in LA.'

'Oh right… You were talking about cocaine?'

'When I was in LA I got in with the wrong crowd and I ended up in a knife fight. I still have the scar. That's when I finally saw sense and cleaned up my act.'

'Do they know about this at Pellier?'

'No. I never felt the need to talk about it officially, and I don't have a criminal record.'

Spencer laughed, 'Perhaps they would see it as a qualification: 'the desired candidate should have a wide experience of life'.'

They drove into Merganserville.

CHAPTER FIVE

At 9.00 on Tuesday, Spencer pushed himself into his next Shakespeare seminar. The subject was *The Tempest*, Shakespeare's last play, and Spencer dearly wished it were his last seminar. He found it hard to concentrate. Each time he glanced at Dani he saw her naked but for a silver wig, pouting and wriggling her butt. He was plagued by the idea that she had recognised him at the strip club, but her demeanour gave nothing away.

There was a little more interest from some of the students as they saw that the relationship between Prospero and Caliban could be seen as one of master and slave, leading on to a discussion of the American legacy of slavery and how the years of the slave trade must cast a pall over any discussion of race to this day. As usual, the debate ran out of steam.

Spencer tried to rally the troops 'Look, let's talk about Shakespeare's use of language. Have you noticed that sometimes he uses prose and at other times he writes in verse? Why?' He looked at Chantal, who answered with some reluctance, 'The aristocrats speak in verse and the comedy characters speak in prose – not that they're funny, in my humble opinion.'

'Okay,' said Spencer, 'but sometimes he will turn that on its head. I mean, Caliban is a monstrous character but sometimes he speaks in verse, and he has one of the most sensitive speeches in the play.' Spencer hoped to impress them by quoting from memory, *'Be not afeared; the isle is full of noises / Sounds and sweet airs, that give delight, and hurt not. / Sometimes a thousand twangling instruments / Will hum about mine ears'*

The students did not look impressed. Spencer ploughed on, 'So he uses language forms to reveal character.' Why had he brought this up? He was starting to bore himself as well as the students.

Dani raised her hand to speak, 'Shakespeare's prose is carefully structured though, isn't it Professor? I mean, you could say it's as structured as the verse.'

'Er, well, er… yes, certainly.'

'I'm rehearsing Portia in the *Merchant of Venice* right now and she has a prose speech full of contrasts. Each line is built round a contrast, like, *'The brain may devise laws for the blood, but a hot temper leaps o'er a cold decree'*, and I've found that you can only make sense of it for the audience if you stress those contrasts and bring out the antithesis as an actor.'

For a tragic second Spencer gaped at her, then managed to speak, 'Er, yes… quite so. Good point. Getting back to *The Tempest*…'

He hid his face behind the book. Why was he making such a mess of this?

At the end of the class, as the students left the room, Spencer handed out a leaflet on the chronology of

Shakespeare's plays. Theo Gustafsson, who had sat glowering in silence throughout, took a photo of the leaflet on his phone; the idea of touching something as antediluvian as a piece of paper seemed beneath him. Again, Spencer noticed the young man's cufflinks. He could see now that the Latin numerals read XIV.

'What's the significance…?' he asked, gesturing vaguely at the cufflinks.

'No significance. No significance at all,' smirked Theo. 'Actually they were a present from my Daddy on my fourteenth birthday.'

Spencer could see he was lying, but why?

To his dismay he saw that Dani had stayed behind.

'Doctor Leyton?'

'Yes Dani.' How was he going to get out of this?

'I just wanted to ask you, respectfully and firmly, to support our protest tomorrow.'

'Well, Dani,' he said, trying to push memories of her naked body out of his thoughts, 'er… I'm still considering the issues on this… but I really must go…'

He hurried out of the door.

At 5.00 Spencer was sitting on a stool at Flanagans, an old-fashioned bar just two blocks from where he lived. It was old-fashioned in the sense that unlike many American bars it had not given itself over to a micro-brewery and an array of craft beers. Spencer sat with a Miller High Life, served just above freezing point.

There were five or six other customers, all of them middle-aged men, all of them staring at the TV screens showing football and basketball. Spencer had been to Flanagan's once before, and after a couple of beers he had repaired to the Mom and Pop diner across the street, where he had eaten a pizza the size of a cartwheel. He planned to do so again.

He was surprised to see Louisa come in through the door. Somehow Spencer had not imagined her frequenting a downmarket Irish bar. She was with a tall wiry man aged about fifty, with greying hair and a moustache.

'Spencer, please come and sit with us,' said Louisa, walking over to a table.

'Well, if I'm not intruding...'

'Don't worry, this is Lloyd and he's not my boyfriend.'

'Not for want of trying,' Lloyd smiled at Spencer, 'but don't tell my wife.'

Settled with drinks, Spencer asked Lloyd if he worked at the university.

'Lord no, I'm not smart enough to do that. I'm a police officer.'

'Lloyd is a lieutenant in the Merganserville police, but I know him from Atlanta. He worked with my husband. He moved up here soon after I did.'

Guess I just got tired of the big city. I prefer a little place like this. Uh… I take it you're from England?'

'Does it show?'

'Is it true the police there don't carry guns?'

'Well, I live in London and you see armed police outside embassies and that kind of thing, but regular patrolmen don't carry guns on a daily basis.'

'So what do they do if they come up against a bad guy with a gun?'

'I suppose a true British police officer will employ British weapons… '

'British weapons?'

'Sarcasm, derision, contempt, heavy irony, satire, mordant wit. And a taser.'

There was silence for a moment, and then Louisa said helpfully, 'Er… Lloyd… I think you'll find this is an example of the British sense of humour.'

Lloyd, though, was laughing already, 'I love it. I love British comedians anyway.'

'Really?' said Spencer, 'Who are your favourites?'

'Oh, all the clever British guys. You know… Stephen Fry, Benny Hill.'

Spencer smiled and nodded with a false enthusiasm. The two names were not quite the juxtaposition he had expected.

Lloyd talked a little about his work in the Merganserville Police Department and explained that – as in many small towns – nearly all the crime occurred in a particular district. In the case of Merganserville this was an area south of downtown known as The Valley. He said it was best avoided at night when drug dealers and prostitutes were out plying their trade.

Spencer asked him if he was involved in policing the Wednesday morning protest.

'No, thank God.'

'You should do though,' said Louisa. 'You'd make a better job of it than some of the cops I've seen there.'

'There are some officers who are a little heavy-handed,' said Lloyd

'And there are some who are violent racist thugs,' countered Louisa.

'Well, I really wouldn't want to comment on that.'

'Everyone else is commenting on it though, aren't they?' said Louisa.

'What do you mean?' asked Spencer.

'I'm not anti-police. I mean, how could I be? But it's gone too far. Most people can see that now.' Louisa sighed and grimaced to herself. 'There are plenty of decent cops like

Lloyd, but you have to understand that things take a long time to change down here. There are people in this town who can remember when the chief of police was also a leading character in the Klan.'

'Really?'

Lloyd nodded, 'That kind of thing was quite common in the South at one time.'

'But do you know any of those people personally?'

'What? Members of the Klan? No, not personally. But they exist – I can tell you that.'

'And did they really have those titles? You know, Imperial Wizard, Grand Dragon...'

Lloyd started to chuckle. 'It's all true. They had a Grand Cyclops, a Grand Titan... it's all a bit like a racialised version of The Hobbit.'

Spencer started to laugh, 'Gandalf of the SS...'

'But,' Louisa broke in, 'you don't have to dress up in a pointy hat to hold those attitudes, and since it's the police we're talking about, it isn't really very funny, is it?'

Lloyd stroked his moustache, looking down at his drink. 'Look, Spencer,' he said, 'this is a small southern town and there's a history, you know, and a suspicion that the African-American population has of the police – with good reason. Even today there are very few black police officers here, and God knows I hear things said at work that you just wouldn't get away with in Atlanta.'

'Do you report it?' asked Louisa, 'Do you call them out on it?'

'If I did, life would be very difficult for me.' He looked uneasily at Spencer. 'Obviously I would not want this to go any further…'

Spencer shook his head, 'You really don't have to worry about that.'

'I don't think I'm going to stay in the job too much longer; now, I'm just keeping my head down.'

'I know I'm not in your position,' said Louisa, 'and this may be easy for me to say, but Edmund Burke wrote that evil prevails when good men do nothing.'

On Wednesday evening Spencer walked a few blocks from his apartment to the 'Chicken Shack'. A sign outside announced that tonight the Jessica Juke Band would be performing. Despite the downhome rootsy name, the Chicken Shack was in fact a well-appointed bar and restaurant with a stage at one end of the room.

Spencer met Louisa at a table inside. 'If you like the blues, you should like Jessica Juke.'

Moments later, the club MC announced, 'Give it up please for the Jessica Juke band!'

Four aging men clambered with some difficulty onto the stage. Certainly they all looked the wrong side of seventy. The drummer clasped his sticks with hands in arthritic knots. The keyboard player had reached a degree of obesity that made it hard for him to reach the keys. The bass player, with grey hair and beard to his waist, looked like Georgia's answer to Ben Gunn. The guitarist, gaunt and adorned with a headband, could have achieved a piratical Keith Richards-style cool – had he not been wearing an orthopaedic boot. None of this seemed to bother the audience, who greeted them with a roar of approval. The musicians found their instruments and their seats – a process that resembled Musical Chairs in a nursing home. Finally, they were ready. The keyboard man counted them in and they swooped into an explosive version of 'Time is Tight' by Booker T. and the MGs. Spencer was impressed; they sounded terrific. After this first instrumental, Jessica Juke took the stage. A black woman, elegant in a black dress, she looked about thirty-five years younger than the musicians.

'Hello,' she said, 'I'm here to sing the blues. The blues are a musical form born of poverty and oppression. So prepare for sixty-five minutes of abject misery.' There was a huge laugh from the audience.

Jessica Juke sang and played harmonica; she sang like Etta James and played harmonica like Little Walter. She opened with Howlin Wolf's 'Smokestack Lightnin', feminising the lyric and turning it into a universal cry for liberation. Spencer was amazed.

The audience was very mixed: black, white, men, women. Liquor laws prevented most students from attending, but there were plenty of people in their twenties. The whole audience seemed to adore her from the first moment she took the stage. She performed seven or eight blues classics , with a couple of jazzy numbers thrown in, acting out each song with dramatic flair but without ever taking it too seriously.

There were several people who were obviously regular fans – mostly the older men. Spencer had the feeling that they turned up to see her every time she performed.

'Any requests?' Jessica Juke shouted. Her musicians groaned in mock horror.

A young man at the front called back, 'Yes – can I have your phone number?'

She called out to the staff, 'Have that boy washed and brought to my dressing room.'

An older man at the front called out, 'One Bourbon, One Scotch, One Beer.'

'Give your drinks order to the waitress,' Jessica returned.

'No, I want to hear 'One Bourbon, One Scotch, One Beer', by John Lee Hooker, recorded in Chicago in 1966 with Lafayette Leake on piano.'

There were some mocking jeers from other members of the audience.

'Marvellous,' said Jessica,' a self-appointed expert. And who, may I ask, recorded the song originally?'

'Willie Dixon?'

'Nope. Amos Milburn. But we're not doing it anyway. We don't want to encourage drinking.'

Another man called out, 'Help Me Baby,'

'Help you with what? Your carburettor? Your tax return?'

'I want to hear 'Help Me Baby', by Sonny Boy Williamson.'

'Sonny Boy Williamson the first or the second?'

'Both of them – no, the second… and I want the version recorded in New York in January 1967.'

'Well that's gonna be a bit difficult because he died in 1965… What key is it in?'

'I'd like to hear it in F Sharp diminished with an augmented third in the second verse.'

Jessica cocked her head on one side and gave the longest pause in history, with audience chuckles turning to guffaws. She then turned to the band and said, 'Let's do it in A'. Without even counting in, they crashed into 'Help Me Baby'. At the end, everyone in the room was on their feet.

When the set was over, Louisa asked Spencer what he thought.

'I think she's fantastic. Brilliant.'

'Good. So do I. I'll bring her over.'

'You know her personally?'

'Friend and colleague for several years. She teaches American History at Pellier. Jessica Juke is just a stage name, of course.'

Louisa linked arms with Jessica and guided her through the crowded room. It was only then that Spencer realised that Jessica was blind.

'Can I get you a drink?' he asked.

'One bourbon, one scotch, one beer. Well I'm not driving am I?' There were chuckles from Spencer and Louisa, 'Actually just make it a beer please.'

Spencer was intrigued. What was it about her conversational voice that was different from the voice she used on stage? She spoke in a confident contralto, but without the need to impose herself on the audience she seemed warmer and more relaxed.

'Are you English?' she asked.

'Er… yes… '

'I was in London two years ago and I loved it. I love the way people speak.' She went into an unconvincing London accent, 'Fair do's boss – I'll get you on the blower.'

'Blower?' returned Spencer, 'don't you mean dog?'

'Dog?'

'Rhyming slang: dog and bone means phone. So, I'll get you on the dog.'

Jessica laughed, 'Yes, rhyming slang, of course.'

'You're not drinking your drink. Go on – get it down your Gregory.'

'Gregory?'

'Gregory Peck – neck.'

Louisa was rolling her eyes.

'I tried to introduce a blank verse style of rhyming slang…
'

Jessica was starting to giggle, 'What, you mean a type of rhyming slang that doesn't actually rhyme?'

'Yes. I thought maybe 'gearbox' could be 'Hampstead Heath'. So you take your car to the mechanic and say, 'Hello guv, take a look at my Hampstead.'

Jessica and Spencer cracked up. Louisa wondered if she'd been transported to a parallel universe where absolutely nothing made any kind of sense.

They talked about their jobs at Pellier and established that Jessica played with her band once or twice a week around the local area. There had been enquiries from managements about recording and touring nationally, but Jessica had explained that she was happy to keep it the way it was. Spencer was lavish in his praise and said that he had briefly played blues harmonica as a teenager.

'Well, if you want to brush up your skills, why don't you come to my class?'

'You teach harmonica?'

'Every Thursday evening at six o'clock. On campus. Ground floor of the music block.'

'You mean the David de Sainte Croix Music Block,' interjected Louisa.

'Oh yes, sorry Dave.'

'Er,,, I don't actually have a harmonica with me,' said Spencer, 'I mean I've got a Marine Band somewhere, but it's back in London.'

'No problem,' Jessica was fumbling in her bag, 'here's a Lee Oskar harmonica. Easier on the lips than a Marine Band. You can keep that. Is that in C?'

'Er… yes it's in the key of C. Look, let me pay you for it; these things are expensive.'

'No, really, it's okay.'

'Well,' said Spencer, 'maybe I can pay you by taking you out for lunch on Friday.'

Did Louisa look a little startled?

'Uh… Friday?' Jessica hesitated. 'Well… yeah, okay… why not?'

'Great. And I'll see you at the harmonica class on Thursday.'

They swapped numbers and Jessica had a ride home with Louisa. Spencer insisted on walking – to the astonishment of the two Americans. All the way home he thought about the woman he had just met. He desperately wanted to see her again as soon as possible.

His wish was granted. At home, he switched on the local news channel and within seconds was watching a report on the protest that morning at the Robert E. Lee statue. Jessica's face was on the screen – here billed as Doctor Jessica Murray. She made a speech to the crowd and gave an impromptu version of 'Strange Fruit' by Billie Holliday. For Spencer, things were falling into place.

****

The play for discussion on Thursday morning was *A Midsummer Night's Dream*. Dani was on the attack from the start, 'When you actually strip it back and look at what's there on the page, this is an appalling play. Theseus and Oberon are unquestioned patriarchs, Helena and Hermia are silly, flighty girls, and when you actually look at what goes on between Titania and Bottom, well… it's just an Elizabethan version of extreme pornography.'

'Is it?' asked Spencer.

'Pardon my language, but what's depicted here – this episode which male scholars tell us is so funny and delightful – is actually a young woman fucking a donkey.'

For the first time ever, Theo Gustafsson started to take an interest.

'Well,' began Spencer, 'it's surely just a man with the head of a donkey… '

'If that's all it is, then it's just totally lame. He has the head of a donkey and the penis of a donkey, doesn't he? That's how we are meant to take it – well it is, isn't it? I don't find that either funny or delightful. If you were found with that kind of thing on your computer, it would be a federal offence. We're also supposed to laugh at all the hilarious confusion caused by the love potion, which, when you think about it, is just an early version of a date-rape drug…'

'Well, okay,' said Spencer, fighting the urge to simply leave the room and not come back, 'but surely the context takes the sting out of it… the world of fairies and the supernatural?'

'Yeah, but that's like, just infantile and pointless as well, isn't it? And totally irrelevant for us today. I'm surprised you haven't noticed that people don't believe in magic anymore.'

'Really?' returned Spencer, his voice a little too loud. 'Well it didn't get in the way for J. K. bloody Rowling, did it?'

There was silence in the room for a long moment.

'Mark? What's your view?'

Mark was wearing a T-shirt with a picture of David Bowie on it. He smiled and said nothing.

Spencer took a deep breath, 'Okay, look… you have chosen to focus on one aspect of the play, but there is surely more to be said. I mean, this play is about transformation, about the power of art, and about the nature of theatre, and... '

'Professor,' said Dani quietly, 'Perhaps you have the luxury of seeing those aspects, and perhaps I don't.'

Spencer stared at Dani. She dropped her gaze.

'Okay, let's take a step back,' said Spencer, 'Let's think about how this play was seen by a previous generation. Take a look at Max Reinhardt's film version from 1935.'

He inserted the DVD and sat back. The students watched the film.

Spencer was on the verge of despair. He had wanted to excite these young people with insights into the greatest poet in the English language, but they seemed to see the Shakespearean canon as nothing more than an arm of oppression.

He gazed at the students in front of him. He wondered if he were the person for the job. He recognised that it was hard for him to be sympathetic to their point of view. Would another teacher fare better? They were all people who could claim membership of some sort of oppressed group, through gender, ethnicity or sexuality. The exception was Theo Gustafsson, who rarely made any kind of contribution.

Spencer was a middle-class, able-bodied, heterosexual white male. Was it impossible for him to feel genuinely, authentically oppressed? Was that the problem here? He recognised injustice all around him, but was he only capable of getting angry on behalf of someone else?

Early on Thursday evening Spencer left his apartment, strolled on to campus, and walked across the car park. He noticed a man standing by a white pick-up, staring into space. Spencer slowed to look at him. The man was in his thirties, and thin. He wore a John Deere baseball cap, and Spencer saw a large knife sheathed at his hip. He really did not look like a student and Spencer wondered what he was doing on campus. The pick-up had Alabama licence plates.

Spencer found his way to the David de Sainte Croix Music Block. As he approached the classroom seven people playing wildly on harmonicas sounded like a group of cats being strangled.

'Sorry I'm a little late – I couldn't find the room. My name's Spencer.'

As usual, his accent caused a flurry of interest. The seven other students all smiled and waved a greeting. One of them, a man in his fifties, elegant in a pale blue seersucker jacket, stood and gave a slight bow. 'My name is Bernard.' (He pronounced it Ber-*nard*) 'I have a cousin in Godalming,' he said.

'Godalming… er… that's nice.'

Jessica took charge of the class.

'Okay Spencer, this class has been running for a few weeks and since you're new to the group we'd better see if you're up to speed with everyone else. Got your harmonica ready? Okay, give me a blow-bend on the 8 hole, and then play a descending second position blues scale in G with a draw bend on the 4 and some diaphragmatic vibrato on the 3. Off you go.'

Spencer stared aghast at the other students. They all started to chuckle.

'Jessica is a wonderful teacher,' offered Bernard, 'but she has a sense of humour of striking aridity.'

'Okay,' said Jessica, 'let's play Happy Birthday instead. It starts with a blow 6.'

She pressed a button on her laptop and the harmonica tablature came up on a screen.

Without too much difficulty they all worked their way through the tune. Spencer looked around the group. There were three women and three men, all of them older than himself. The students all had basic entry-level instruments – except for Bernard, who had six Hohner Meisterklasse harmonicas in different keys, each costing over $100, all tucked neatly into a custom-made walnut and velvet case. The class worked through various simple exercises, and Spencer was surprised to find how much he could remember since he'd last played years earlier. Occasionally Jessica would break off from the exercises to play a brief clip from one of the masters of blues harmonica. Sonny Terry, Jimmy Reed and Paul Butterfield were all featured. After each one Bernard would try to impress the class with his knowledge of their work, listing obscure vinyl records that he had bought on trips to specialist dealers in Memphis and New Orleans. Jessica always managed to close him down tactfully but firmly.

At the end of the class Jessica called on each student to improvise for a verse. Spencer found he could remember the 12-bar blues structure accurately enough to sound reasonable, and the others all managed pretty well. Except Bernard, who blew into the harmonica with maximum volume and minimum musicality.

As they were packing up, Louisa appeared at the door, 'Hello Spencer, how did it go?'

'Here's my chauffeur,' said Jessica, 'and he did just fine. Actually he was Robin.'

Louisa looked bemused, 'Robin?'

'Robin Hood. Good.' She giggled at Louisa, 'See you for lunch tomorrow Spencer.'

Back at his apartment, Spencer watched the news on TV, as he usually did. He felt a little homesick and wondered when any of the American networks would show a story concerning a country other than the USA. And he thought about Jessica. Not only was she beautiful and gifted – she was also, he now realised, a great teacher.

He sat at his lap-top and tried to Skype his daughter Rosie. She did not pick up. He went to bed and thought back to the time when the children were very young, before his marriage to Sarah began to corrode. They were his happiest memories, and he clutched them like precious jewels.

CHAPTER SIX

The following day Spencer and Jessica met in an Italian place just off campus. Jessica was already sitting down when he arrived.

'Have you just put out a cigarette?' she asked as he sat down.

'Er… I was smoking outside.'

'I hate the smell. It's overpowering. It sticks to your clothes.'

'Oh… er… sorry.'

There was an awkward pause.

'They do say,' tried Spencer, 'that in America today there are places where it's legal to have a loaded gun but not a lit cigarette.'

'Yes, well, you've heard of passive smoking?'

'Yes, but I've also heard of passive shooting in the sense of innocent people being caught in the crossfire. Shall I go out and come back in again? We seem to have got off on the wrong foot.'

Jessica smiled. 'No Spencer, it's okay. I just hate the smell of smoking. Here – have a dab of Chanel and that'll solve the problem.'

A bottle of perfume appeared. Spencer did as he was asked and they ordered pasta and salad.

'How long have you been playing harmonica?' asked Spencer.

'I've played since I was a child. Playing seriously with the band – that's the last seven years, I guess. The teaching is much more recent. I had so many requests I could no longer ignore them.'

'I enjoyed the class; I love the blues. America's greatest gift to the world.'

'It wasn't a gift, Spencer – it was stolen.'

'You mean stolen by white people?'

'They were the ones who made the money out of it.'

'Yes, but then we white English boys gave it back in the 1960s. American radio was so segregated back then – I am sure you know this – white kids in America didn't know anything about it till the Stones and the Yardbirds and all the others brought it back.'

'Can blue men sing the whites?' cracked Jessica.

'Look, Jessica, you're a real blues singer and you're from the place where the blues was born, so I don't think I'm going to try to give you a lecture on this, but in my opinion the blues is not about your skin. It's about your heart. As far as I'm concerned, music has no colour. The blues is a universal language. Music belongs to everyone.'

'Yeah, but who gets the royalties?

'Well, the Stones were always good about that – crediting the song to the right songwriter.'

'You could say that the blues belongs to black Americans because they created it.'

'Then why are you teaching it to white people?'

'I deliberately teach them to play badly,' said Jessica, giggling.

'Jessica, I will give up my harmonica when you pry it from my cold dead fingers.'

Jessica laughed.

'I saw you on TV,' said Spencer, 'at the protest at the statue.'

'Will you be coming to join us?'

Spencer prodded his pasta a little awkwardly, 'I don't want to get deported… I don't know… I feel this doesn't involve me.'

'At the risk of sounding pompous, I think it involves anyone who believes in free speech. The police are suppressing valid peaceful protest. You see, Spencer, this black anger is not directed at white people in general; it's against City Hall and the police. So the violence is not black on white so much as black on blue. But around here we have these white supremacist groups who want to stir it up into a race war.'

She took a sip of water, 'You can say that racist groups like that are part of the Old South, but they keep the fires burning. Everyone should have the right to feel safe, and there are times when I really don't. Then again, I often think that these Neo Nazis are not driven by racial hatred so much as a twisted version of masculinity.' She smiled at him, 'Spencer, I would be very pleased if you could attend the protest, and I know it would go down well with the students. I can't see that you'll get deported for doing so, and the truth is we need more white men to stand with us. Speaking out at demonstrations is not going to give us a perfect world by next Tuesday, but it chips away at the power structure.'

They finished lunch, and Spencer insisted on paying the bill.

'Thank you Spencer.'

'You know, Jessica, I read somewhere that the population of Merganserville is about 40 per cent African-American, but walking around the area near the university you would never think that.'

'Do you mainly see white people?'

'Well, yes. Not just the customers in the stores, but the people serving them as well.'

'Not ten minutes' walk from here, I could show you a neighbourhood where there are no white people at all. Are you saying it would be different in a town in England?'

'A town of this size in England probably wouldn't have a black population. People of African heritage live in large cities in Britain. That's maybe not so true of other minorities, like the Indians and the Pakistanis, but then you get a whole lot of different issues with them. I've heard that half of all African-Caribbean people in Britain live in inner London, so you wonder how much integration has really taken place.'

'I know things aren't perfect where you come from, but here in America race is the Elephant in the Room. It's in every discussion, and we're just not at ease with ourselves over it.'

'Well in Britain some would say social class is the Elephant in the Room. It seems to underlie everything.'

Spencer thought carefully about what he was going to say next. He told himself not to move too fast.

Trying to make it sound like a casual question, Spencer spoke, 'I don't feel I've seen much of Merganserville at all yet. Could you perhaps show me round tomorrow?'

'Look… Spencer… I have things to do tomorrow.'

'Yes of course, that's fine.' Disappointment sat in the pit of his stomach.

She thought for a while.

'Okay look. How about I take an hour out of my schedule? We can go for tea and cakes.'

'That's great. I would like that.'

Walking home, the place seemed very foreign. In London, every neighbourhood held memories and associations for him, but there could be none of that here. He was just a stranger in town. He thought of his friends at home and he thought of his children. But then there was hardly an hour went by when he did not think of his children. He had said before he left London that eight weeks away was not long, but in fact it was the longest he had ever been apart from them. Eight weeks might seem short before it begins, but once it has begun it may seem like eternity.

****

The following day, Jessica was sitting on the porch when he pulled up outside her house.

'Are you ready to go?' he asked.

'Cor blimey, yes me old china. Stone the crows, I don't Adam and Eve it. Are you 'avin' a giraffe?'

'Good grief,' muttered Spencer.

'Did you not realise you were having tea with Dick Van Dyke?'

'I think the politically correct version is Penis Van Lesbian.'

Jessica laughed in spite of herself, 'If you tell any more jokes as old as that, I'll make you pay for the cakes.'

'I have an environmentally responsible sense of humour: I like to recycle old jokes.'

They drove downtown and parked the car on a stretch of Main Street that consisted largely of red brick buildings going back to the 1850s. It had much more character than most of what Spencer had seen of the town. He examined the billboard at the Grand Theatre. There seemed to be no upcoming professional productions: just a series of 'open mic' nights. There were separate nights for jazz, blues, poetry, comedy and magic. 'No Need To Book!' said the billboard, 'Just Turn Up!' There were opportunities to watch people demonstrating incompetence at playing music, talking aloud and pulling rabbits out of hats. Spencer reflected that if this made for a cheap night out for the customers it was even cheaper for the theatre management.

The Yellow Dog Café was the kind of place that sold vegan soup and thirty types of organic fairtrade coffee.

'Why "Yellow Dog?"' asked Spencer as they went in.

'It's just a jokey reference to the Yellow Dog Democrats. They were people who would vote for a yellow dog before they would vote for a Republican.'

Most of the customers seemed to be students and several of them recognised Jessica.

'Good afternoon, Doctor Murray, what can I get you?' said the waitress as she placed the obligatory iced water on the table.

'Good afternoon, Harriet,' replied Jessica. She turned to Spencer, 'This is Harriet. She's one of my best students.'

'I bet you say that to all the waitresses here,' smiled the young woman.

'Of course. It guarantees that I get good service. Now, do you have any cucumber sandwiches for my English friend?'

'Alas, Doctor Murray, there were no cucumbers at the market today, not even for ready money.'

'In that case we'll have a pot of English Breakfast tea and two of the large warm fudge brownies.'

'Did she really just quote Oscar Wilde?' asked an impressed Spencer as the waitress left them.

'Some of our students actually read books. Just not many.'

'Not many students or not many books?'

'Both.'

They drank their tea and Jessica talked about her work. She had been teaching American History at Pellier for ten years. Her PhD centred on the period of reconstruction after the Civil War. She enjoyed teaching, but like all teachers hated the paperwork; when it all became too stressful she had her singing and her harmonica to keep her sane. Spencer said little. He was happy to listen to Jessica. Sunlight streamed into the café. He loved the way the corner of her mouth crinkled when she smiled. He had not felt this way for a very long time.

Back on Main Street, Spencer was conscious of the glances they received. In some cases they were stares rather than glances.

'Let's go the cemetery,' said Jessica

'What do you have in mind – a suicide pact?'

'Spencer… do you ever take anything seriously?'

'Not if I can avoid it.'

'Well, the cemetery is a beautiful place. It's the most peaceful place. Which is ironic, because it only exists because of war.'

They walked a few blocks to the Merganserville Military Cemetery.

'Let me hold on tight to you,' said Jessica, 'Some of the ground is rough.'

Jessica held her white cane in her right hand and took hold of Spencer's arm with her left.

'Do you always carry the cane when you go out?' asked Spencer.

'Well, I don't carry it when I'm doing a gig, but mostly the rest of the time. I always have it at college because it's very useful for hitting the students.'

The cemetery was large, with room for several hundred graves, overshadowed by a line of poplars running along one side. They walked amongst the headstones and Spencer was struck by the tranquillity of the place and by the beauty of the water oaks dotted around the graveyard. They were just three blocks from Main Street but there was no sound of traffic.

'Are people still being buried here?' asked Spencer.

'No, not for many years, and the majority of the graves are for Confederate Soldiers.'

'Are there any Union graves?

'There were a few, but they were moved just after the Civil War. There's another cemetery just outside town, which is just as well, because I would not be totally comfortable being shoved in with the forces of the Confederacy.'

'You're not planning on dying quite yet, I hope…'

She laughed and gripped his arm. Was she warming to him a little?

The cemetery was immaculately kept, with a tiny Confederate flag by each soldier's plot. He read aloud the inscriptions on some of the gravestones: 'Corporal Jasper Bates. 10th Texas Infantry'; 'Sergeant John Shepherd. 1st Georgia Infantry. "The South Shall Rise Again".'

'What does that even mean?' he asked her.

'There are some who would say it means the South will rise and split off from the rest of the country. Have you heard of the Confederate Nation?'

'No.'

'They are one of many white nationalist groups but they actually think the South can be an independent nation in the foreseeable future. In the meantime they keep busy hating Black people, hating Jews, hating communists, homosexuals, and all the usual targets. I'm not sure that they pose a real threat, or if maybe they're just a bunch of nutjobs.'

'Would you be likely to have any contact with them?'

'I used to teach a boy called Theo Gustafsson, and I'm pretty sure he was a member of the Confederate Nation'

'Theo Gustafsson? He's one of my students.'

'What do you make of him?'

'Well – a nutjob actually.'

'He took my 'Legacy of the Civil War' module. The first clue was that he kept referring to the 'War Between the States'.

'But that's technically accurate isn't it?'

'Well, no, not really, because it was all one country. Nowadays the term 'War Between the States' is used by supporters of the Lost Cause. They also like to call it the War of Northern Aggression. You see, Spencer, there's plenty of revisionism about the War. The fact is the Civil War really was about slavery – pure and simple – but so many people want to deny that.'

They walked on in silence for a while. It seemed to Spencer that even on the smoother ground Jessica was holding on to him tightly. Then suddenly,

'Oh no…' said Spencer

'You've just seen the slave plot, haven't you?'

'Yes.'

'How does it look right now?'

'It looks terrible. How many…?'

'There are fourteen slaves buried here, but they don't all have headstones and there are no names anywhere.'

There was a placard explaining that this was the slave plot, but the plot itself was just a patch of ground with a few small gravestones, one of them tilted at an angle. Spencer bent down to retrieve the wrapper of a candy-bar that had blown onto the plot.

'It's unkempt… it's wretched…'

'Indignity in death as well as life,' said Jessica.

They stood for a while, close together. There was a great contrast between the graves of the slaves and the graves of those who died fighting to preserve their slavery.

'Do you think racism started with slavery or the other way round?' asked Spencer.

'Oh Lord… you could get a PhD thesis out of that one. Human beings have enslaved each other for thousands of years. It certainly did not begin with the Atlantic slave trade, and there have been many examples of people enslaving members of their own ethnic group. So you can't speak of an endemic connection between racism and slavery, but it is also pretty damned obvious that the one will support the other. If you dehumanise a group, it makes it easier to mistreat them. Just as an example, you have the Nazis referring to Jews as rats.'

'I noticed something the other day. Theo Gustafsson has cufflinks with the number fourteen in Latin numerals. Is that significant?'

She paused and cocked her head on one side, 'The Latin is not significant. That's probably just his affectation. But the number fourteen… that's very significant.'

'What does it mean?'

'It's the fourteen words...'

'What?'

'It's a white supremacist slogan, 'We must secure the existence of our people and a future for white children.'

'Bloody hell.' Spencer thought for a while. 'So I have a neo-Nazi in my class. I can't refuse to teach him, can I?'

'No, you really can't, but I think you should be aware of what he represents.'

At the centre of the cemetery, underneath a huge oak tree, was a plaque. Spencer read it to Jessica: 'To those Heroes of the South who Died in a Sacred Cause.'

They stood in silence. Jessica still hung onto him. On a chilly afternoon he was aware of the warmth of her body.

'They died in an evil cause,' said Spencer, 'but does that make the soldiers themselves evil? I mean, how do you acknowledge their sacrifice without glorifying it?'

'The Vietnam War was an unpopular war by the time the troops came home,' said Jessica. 'And the veterans were not treated with much respect – and that wasn't right.'

'I don't know what the answer is.'

'It's getting a bit cold now, isn't it Spencer? Perhaps you could take me home.'

They walked back through town, reached the car, and drove towards the university area.

'Well, there's the statue,' said Spencer. 'What do they call this park, anyway?'

'Lee Park – wouldn't you know it?'

'This thing about pulling it down… I'm just not sure. You can never rewrite history. It's there. It's part of the past. You know, some people wanted to destroy the house in Austria where Hitler was born. What are they trying to say? That he never existed?'

'Spencer… honestly… you just don't get it. I don't care if people tell me that Lee was personally opposed to slavery. It's like saying that Hitler liked animals. That statue is a daily affront to black people, just as for women the way our bodies are used for advertising is a daily affront. And a white man can never really understand that because there is no equivalent.'

'Well okay,' said Spencer, 'but can't you just let them have their statue and ignore it? I'm sure that for some white people it's just nostalgia.'

'Yes, as long as you accept that for a black American there can be no nostalgia. How can we look back fondly on *any* period of American history? We can't. A white person experiences it differently, and that's what I am talking about – daily experience. I mean I'm not sure that a discussion ever really changes people's views, but personal experience of life does.'

Spencer stopped the car for a moment to look again at the statue.

'Look, I'm involved in political action,' Jessica said, 'because it changes laws. Life is better for black people in this country than it was fifty years ago, and that has come about through legislation. But does political action change people's hearts and minds? I doubt it. Most white people think they are superior to me because I'm black…'

'No but if you…'

'…And men interrupt women because they think they're superior.'

'Well, we walk through different worlds, I know that.'

'But it is far more than that, Spencer, because of the standing you are given by the rest of the world, or at least by that part of the world that consists of white men who happen to be the people with the power.'

'I honestly can't say that I feel powerful.'

'Well, I mean, exactly… I mean that is *exactly* the point. You are not going to be aware of it, but it is there – every minute of your life, and all I am saying is that you, like any white man, should acknowledge your position and not get defensive when women and black people and disabled people and everyone who isn't a white man… oh, and let's not forget sexual minorities – have I left anyone out? – don't get defensive when others want a place at the table.'

Spencer was not enjoying the discussion and wished they could talk about harmonicas instead.

They drove past the front gate of the university and Jessica spoke again, 'When it comes to the protest at the statue, mostly I'm preaching to the choir, and I accept that. It's very important that I make a stand, and that it is a public stand. I don't claim to work miracles. No matter what I do, white men will still see themselves as the norm, and every other group as a kind of aberration.'

'But is that because you are a minority in this country, and in my country come to that? I mean, it would be different if we were in Africa.'

'Honestly, Spencer, you really do say some ridiculous things.'

Somewhat taken aback, Spencer said nothing. He was in a foreign land in more ways than one. He realised that he rarely had this sort of conversation back home – he rarely needed to.

Jessica sounded a little tired, as if she had gone over this ground many times before. 'If we were dropped down in almost any African country you can name, you would be part of a postcolonial elite, and anyway do you really think Africa is big on gender equality? Look, you cannot possibly understand that your situation is underpinned by power in a way that mine never will be. That is the point…'

She chuckled to herself. 'Goddammit! You really have got me going haven't you? Don't get me wrong – I don't go round feeling angry all the time. I just avoid the assholes who make life difficult.'

The afternoon light was fading as they reached Jessica's home. She lived in a small, one-storey house, two blocks from campus. The front door opened onto a living room/kitchen area. Spencer noticed how clean and tidy everything was. Cooking utensils hung on hooks, arranged in order of size.

'Do you have a housekeeper?' he asked.

'Yes, a Mexican lady called Catalina comes every morning. She's terrific. Of course, it's okay for me to exploit Hispanics. They came of their own accord: we came in chains. I am joking.' She pressed a button on a remote control and music occurred in the background: quietly, BB

King's guitar was weaving its spell. Jessica hung up her coat and sat down on the sofa.

'I'm tired,' she muttered.

Spencer sat next to her and slipped his arm round her shoulders.

Jessica froze. 'Take your arm away. Right now.'

Embarrassed, Spencer retreated hurriedly to the other end of the sofa.

'Sorry. I misread the signs.'

'That's okay, it's not a crime. I like you, but... don't take things for granted, okay? And... also... you really don't understand how things work here.'

'Other people's prejudice prevents you from doing what you want?'

'I said I liked you. I didn't say I wanted you. There's a difference. Jesus – have I got to jump into bed with any white guy who tells me to?'

'I did not say that.' Spencer's voice was a little too loud.

'But you're assuming I'm available to you. You're prepared to grant me the honour of having sex with you... is that it?' Jessica's voice was rising in volume too.

'I don't think that's fair.'

'Or is it because I'm blind? Am I supposed to be grateful?'

'I'm sorry, really, but I wasn't thinking anything like that.'

'I cannot read your mind, but I feel like I've been here before.'

'You haven't been here with me before. Are white men all the same? Who's making assumptions now?'

'In my experience white men's expectations don't change that much. Okay, maybe you're different. Maybe you're absolutely fucking unique.'

Spencer stood up. 'I'm sorry. I've offended you. I didn't mean to. I'd better go.'

Jessica was silent. She shook her head, wearily.

'Don't get me wrong. I think you're a nice guy, but you are totally out of your depth.'

'I am sorry, really I am, but I…' Spencer tailed off. He felt very foolish. 'I would just like to get to know you better, if that's okay.'

'Spencer, I said I liked you and I do. Just don't pressure me, okay?'

Spencer drove a few blocks to his apartment, going through the kind of emotions he hadn't experienced since he was aged sixteen. His phone beeped. It was a text from Jessica, 'Come on Monday. We can take a walk round campus.'

CHAPTER SEVEN

'If we walk all the way round the path at the edge of campus, that is exactly one-and-a-half miles. So that's a brisk twenty-minute walk,' said Jessica, stepping out purposefully, holding onto Spencer's right arm with her left.

Any hopes of a brisk walk were soon dashed. Every few paces a student would greet Jessica and engage her in conversation. Spencer was struck by the respect shown to her by everyone they met. When they did have a chance to talk, Jessica explained how her day-to-day life was facilitated by a support system of friends who lived within a few minutes' drive. The university security staff could be summoned in the event of a crisis.

'But in event of an emergency you'd call 911?'

'Yes, certainly, but there are some police officers who would not lift a finger to help me. I'm seen as a trouble-maker. Which is what I am, actually.'

'What do you mean?'

'A few months ago I was part of a series of protests against racism in the local police force, so I don't have too many friends there.'

They sat for a while by some rose gardens at the north end of the campus. It was the middle of the afternoon on a warm day. 'I love it here,' she said, 'I love the smell of the roses. Are they pink?'

'I'd say they were pink, yes. How well can you see them?'

'Hardly at all, but they smell pink.'

'Could you… er… tell me how much you see?'

'Well, I can see that you feel awkward about asking me, but I'm cool, really. You see, I am what's called legally blind. I can distinguish shapes, I can see some colour. I can tell day from night. Very few blind people live in darkness.'

She paused, feeling the sun on her face.

'If I look at the sky on a sunny day I see the same blue that you do. Other colours, when there is less light, I'm not so sure. Also, I sense things differently from you. It's real hard to explain, but I can "find" colours through my nose and my ears. I "smell" colours, "hear" colours.'

'Do you mean you have synaesthesia?'

'No – well, I've never been diagnosed. You know Duke Ellington had that? No, I think it's just my way of seeing. We all see things differently.'

'Do we? I mean I don't feel the wind on my face and see a certain colour.'

Jessica chuckled to herself. 'People see things differently in ways that are actually much more important. If a young black woman sees a bunch of young black men on the street she might check them out to see if any of them are her friends. Or she might just check them out for boyfriend material. If a cop sees a bunch of young black men, he sees a crime that's about to be committed.'

Spencer laughed, 'So the answer is… more blind cops?'

'There is one rather strange thing, though…'

'What's that?' said Spencer.

'I can hear the grass grow….'

'Really?'

'…when I drop acid. Hahaha.'

'Yes, very funny.'

 'Close your eyes, Spencer. Listen.'

'Listen to what?'

'Just listen.'

Spencer closed his eyes and listened for five or six minutes.

'So what did you hear?'

'Well, after a little while I could hear you breathing. I could hear some kind of electrical hum from a building somewhere. I heard a few cars on the road by campus. There are some children playing a little while off. That's it.'

'You didn't hear any birdsong?'

'Yes, birds. I heard birds.'

'I can hear three types of bird, and one of them is a blue jay. Listen for a moment. It's quite a harsh call and it's quite close… There it is.'

'I'm sorry Jessica: I am not very good on birds.'

'Oh, don't worry… I've trained myself to identify birdsong. I sit here listening quite a lot, as you can imagine.'

'Do you mind if I smoke?'

'I've got to be honest Spencer: I really do mind. It blots out my sense of smell.'

'Okay, no problem.'

They sat for a while. He was surprised by how comfortable he felt with her. Jessica, though, seemed to have no repose: she always wanted to be up and ready for whatever was coming next. He wished she would relax with him.

'Spencer, do you mind if we go back now? I really need to practise the harmonica.'

'Yes, of course… do you play every day?'

'Yes, at least twenty minutes and I get antsy if I don't. Let's go.'

Jessica practised the harmonica and Spencer listened. She showed him how she could play in four different keys on one harmonica. 'In practice, though, I only use two.'

'That's first and second position?'

'Good. You're learning. Actually, I do use third position occasionally. It's good when you play in a minor key.'

'I thought you never played the blues in a minor key.'

'Oh, some things work in that way. Do you know 'Saint James Infirmary'?

'Oh yes.'

'Well, I play that one in D minor.'

She played through the tune gently and slowly.

'It's a simple tune, but you do have to bend a couple of the notes.'

'I'm still struggling with that.'

'On the low notes you bend by sucking and on the high notes you bend by blowing. It means you lower the note by a semi-tone.'

'So how do you do it?'

'It's quite hard to explain. It's a sort of gulping action. For most people it's a matter of trial and error, and then suddenly it comes together. Don't rush it.'

Spencer tried to bend a note, without much success.

'It will come. Then, when you've got the hang of that, you move on to double-bends where you lower the note by a whole tone.

Jessica pressed a button on her laptop and a 12-bar blues backing track started

'Go on, here's a harmonica in the key of C. Have a blow.'

'I can't play in front of an expert.' Suddenly his harmonica playing was taking on an importance that he did not welcome.

''Course you can. You do in my class.'

'That's different, somehow…'

'Go on. Try second position.'

Hunched forward in an arm-chair, Spencer riffed his way through a couple of verses. Jessica seemed very impressed.

'You've got a really nice tone, and you've got a good sense of the blues structure.'

'Thank you,' Spencer said shyly. He was genuinely relieved. He was used to being the teacher rather than the student.

'Have you always loved blues?' he asked.

'Yes, My Daddy had blues records, so I grew up listening to blues and gospel. When I was twelve, the other kids were listening to hip hop and I was listening to "Muddy Waters".'

'I suppose I started listening to blues when I was fifteen. I think it was Elmore James that hit me first.'

'I've always thought it was strange that white Englishmen got into it so much.'

'I know. Usually middle-class white boys too, not kids from the mean streets. Eric Clapton and Mick Jagger were from the leafy suburbs. So was I, for that matter. Maybe that was it. A totally different world.' He stretched his legs out in front of him. 'The blues were exotic, yes, and there was the sensuality of the music. When I heard Slim Harpo singing "'I'm a King Bee"' and John Lee Hooker singing "Crawling King Snake", I knew they weren't singing about Natural History.'

Jessica leant over and kissed him on the cheek, 'I've got some work to do now, but I'll see you at the harmonica class.'

'Thanks for the extra lesson.'

****

On Tuesday morning Spencer was labouring his way through his seminar on *Romeo and Juliet*. Dani was staring out of the window. Mary was on the verge of sleep. Was this his fault? He hated to think that he had let them down.

Desperate to liven things up, he invited the students to imagine how modern productions might set the play to reflect modern conflicts, as 'West Side Story' had done. Chantal suggested a production set in modern Georgia, with a white Romeo and a black Juliet.

'Good suggestion Chantal,' said Spencer, with an enthusiasm the suggestion did not really deserve. 'Of course, it's a localised conflict. What I mean is… well, where I come from, inter-racial dating is far more accepted. In modern London such a thing would not create conflict. Seeing a white man with a black woman would not be considered remarkable.'

Was there some smirking and averting of eyes? Was his friendship with Jessica out in the public arena already?

He felt uncomfortable and tried to open the discussion up.

'So, are love stories tragic through internal conflict – or is it usually the pressure of outside forces that creates the tragedy? The star-crossed lovers who cannot escape their fate, how would that work in a modern setting of the play? To put it another way: what is the modern equivalent to the forces of fate?'

Spencer was amazed to see Theo Gustafsson raise his hand. He hardly ever made any comment. He stared intently at Spencer, choosing his words, his voice cold.

'Well Doctor Leyton, I would say that a modern equivalent to fate could be punishment for transgression. If, for example, a foreigner enters a community that has a well-established code of values and generally accepted standards of honour and decency and if that person then flouts those codes in a particularly flagrant and distasteful way, well… you could say that person has brought fate down upon their head. You could say that person is going to get what's coming to them as surely as the dawn.'

Theo Gustafsson stared at Spencer and Spencer stared back. There was a long silence. Spencer was starting to feel sick.

'You see, Doctor Leyton, it's just an example.'

'Yes, yes of course. Thank you Theo. Thank you for your contribution.'

****

He did not tell Jessica that he was going, but on Wednesday morning he made his way to Lee Park. Clearly some sort of arrangement had been made, because there was no ring of riot police around the statue this week. There were though, several patrol cars parked around the perimeter of the park, along with a couple of larger vehicles packed with officers in riot gear. Spencer decided to keep a low profile, staying at a distance from the statue.

Apart from Jessica, he did not recognise any of the speakers. There were three of them, all apparently students. They all stressed the need for calm and the futility of meeting violence with violence. One of them evoked the spirits of Martin Luther King and Gandhi.

The protest remained calm. It was only as people began to drift away that Spencer noticed a group of white men a few yards behind him. They were mostly in their thirties and forties, and several were filming the protest on camera phones. One of them had a SLR camera with a long lens, and he appeared to be photographing individual members of the crowd. Spencer suddenly recognised the youngest member of the group. It was Theo Gustafsson. The group saw Spencer and turned their lenses towards him. 'There is nothing to be afraid of,' said Spencer to himself, but no one was fooled, least of all Spencer. He walked out of the park.

At the harmonica class, Jessica took them through their scales and tried to get them all playing simple tunes from memory, followed by some blues improvisation.

There was a short break in the middle of the class and Spencer chatted to a woman called Anne.

'My husband was a serious harmonica player back in the day, when we lived in Atlanta. He played with some famous blues musicians back then. He played with the Allman Brothers – just jam sessions, y'know. He didn't record with people like that, but he had his own band at one time.'

'What was his name?'

'His name for music was Jack Harp, but his real name was Jacob Haimovich. He said he felt that Blues and Jews didn't quite go together.'

Spencer laughed. 'I would disagree. What about Mike Bloomfield? I think Peter Green is Jewish, and Muddy Waters said that apart from the blacks the Jews were the only people who could play the blues.'

'Oh anyone can play the blues. You just need blood in your veins,' said Anne.

'Does he still play now?'

She looked away.

'I lost dear Jacob last year…'

'I'm sorry.'

'It was his heart. It was very sudden. It has been difficult. I just miss him so much… all the time. If you make someone the centre of your world, then when they go…'

Anne looked down at the Hohner Special 20 Harmonica in her hands.

'He had so many harmonicas. Every key, every model, collectors' pieces. He loved them. I couldn't bear to see them just lying in a drawer, so I signed up for Jessica's class. She's just been wonderful to me…'

Anne was silent for a moment.

'When I play, it's almost as if Jacob is alive again. It's silly I know, because we were not religious Jews. He didn't believe in an afterlife. Although I do, actually.'

'He believed in the blues,' offered Spencer, 'and I am sure he would be proud of you.'

He blew gently into his harmonica for a moment, improvising a tune. 'For me,' he said, 'and I think this is why I love the blues – for me the theme that runs through the music is a sense of loss and a desire for a new beginning.'

'Well, this class has given me a new beginning, I know that.'

Jessica called for their attention and resumed the class. 'Okay, well you all know how to get a vibrato effect by using your hands, but any decent harmonica player should be able to play with vibrato using their diaphragm. No, I am not asking you to play the harmonica using a contraceptive device.' The quip earned some dutiful chuckles. 'No, the diaphragm is a thin, skeletal muscle that sits at the base of the chest.' She patted her stomach to demonstrate. 'So let's try some rapid panting using the diaphragm. Okay, off you go, and don't feel disheartened if you can't do it immediately. You might find yourself running out of breath. Like so many things it comes in time.'

Jessica came round the class, checking everyone's diaphragmatic breathing by placing her hand on their stomachs, muttering words of encouragement and correction as she did so. Was it Spencer's imagination or did she spend longer touching him than she did with the other students? Did she stand more closely to him than she did with the others?

Everyone was packing up at the end of the class when Louisa arrived to give Jessica a ride home.

'Do you folks want to come to a gig in Atlanta tomorrow night?' asked Jessica

'Not if it's a blues gig,' Louisa said emphatically.

Spencer was surprised, 'Are you not a blues fan, Louisa?'

'Oh, don't get me wrong…I mean, I love to hear Jessica play, but that's different. The blues generally – well, good heavens – you get some old guy complaining about how he's woken up and can't find his shoes. Why didn't he put them in a place where he would be able to find them? And what does he do then? He simply repeats that he's just woken up and can't find his shoes. As if telling us once wasn't enough.'

'You should speak to Walt,' laughed Spencer, 'he's of the same school of thought.'

'Well Spencer, unless you've joined Louisa in the ranks of the Philistines, perhaps you'd like to come. The fact is that I want to see one of my former harmonica students, a young man called Tommy Coupland. He was in the class two years ago, and after the first six weeks I realised I had nothing left to teach him. So he moved down to Atlanta and formed a band. They're called the Baton Rouge Blues Band. I don't like the name much because none of them are from Baton Rouge. They're doing a gig in Atlanta and we can go, if you like.'

'Yes… I would like that.'

Spencer walked home feeling confused. Was the night out in Atlanta to be thought of as a 'date'? Was she interested him in that way? He had misread the signs once and he did not want to make the same mistake again.

****

'I'll take you through some of the nice parts of town,' said Jessica as they came into Atlanta, 'don't bother with GPS.'

Despite her lack of sight, she was able to give Spencer surprisingly accurate directions.

'Are we on West Paces Ferry Road?'

'Er… yes.'

'Good. Take a right at the Chevron gas station.'

They drove through the leafy, expensive neighbourhood of Buckhead. To Spencer it looked like Dulwich on steroids. They headed downtown and parked the car outside a place called 'Bobby Lee's Blues Bar'. At the door of the club, Jessica's $20 bill was refused. 'Your money's no good here, Miss Jessica'. The doorman shouted over his shoulder, 'Hey, Bobby Lee, look who's here.' Bobby Lee, a larger-than-life individual in zoot suit and Stetson came through from the back.

'Well, look who it is,' he grinned, picking Jessica up in a bear-hug, 'it sure is good to see you.'

'This is my friend Spencer. He's over from England.'

Spencer endured a breath-challenging embrace, 'Welcome to Atlanta,' said Bobby Lee, 'Hey, we had John Mayall here last month. He's from England. He's playing great and he's even older than I am.'

Bobby Lee gestured to a young woman behind the desk. 'Shelley, can you find a table for Jessica and tell the barman that she don't pay for no drinks.'

Jessica held up a hand in protest, 'Bobby Lee, you don't have to do this…'

'I don't have to do anything I don't want to do… and anyway I'm just repaying a debt. You taught that boy Tommy how to play harp and this place is full every time he comes here. So I guess I owe you a few hundred bucks.'

On the way to their table, Jessica was stopped at every step by old acquaintances, many of them grateful former students. Spencer smiled to see her enjoying the attention. For once, she seemed to be letting her guard down.

The Baton Rouge Blues Band took to the stage, to loud applause and shouts of approval. They kicked off with a thunderous version of Robert Johnson's classic 'Crossroads Blues'. A song that could be taken as an account of an unsuccessful day's hitch-hiking here became a frenzied self-interrogation on the choices we make in life: some are good and some are very very bad. Tommy Coupland sang lead, his voice closer to Robert Plant than Big Bill Broonzy, and in the first instrumental break his harmonica intertwined with the guitarist's riffs, squealing blow-bends at the high end of a G harp. In his second solo he doubled down, spilling dozens of notes like tiny pearls through each phrase, before swooping and crooning on long bends through the middle octave.

A diatonic harmonica has ten holes and twenty reeds: twenty tiny strips of metal made to vibrate with the player's breath. How could something so flimsy produce one of the most exciting sounds in music? Tommy Coupland evoked the sound of train whistles on lonely southern nights, of work-hollers on Mississippi plantations, of electric bands on the South Side of Chicago. It was the sound that spelt salvation to the white boys of Dartford and Epsom, clear, cold water in the desert that was Tin Pan Alley and emasculated British pop music. It was the sound that set their souls on fire.

Everyone was on their feet, dancing wildly. This was how the blues was meant to be heard, thought Spencer, just as it was heard in the juke-joints of the 1930s, when the music fuelled dancing, drinking and partying. The main difference, of course, was that here in modern Atlanta, 'The City Too Busy To Hate', everyone in the room was white – except for Jessica, who was spinning around Spencer like an intoxicated hornet. She grabbed hold of him and wrenched him into a jitterbug. Spencer had never been a dancer, but right now he wasn't being given a choice. Jessica's dancing was graceful and energised, and the music seemed to transport her to another plane. The sound seemed to shimmer through her body. The band played just one slow song, a stunning version of Jimmy Oden's 'Going Down Slow'. To Spencer's surprise Jessica took him in a tight embrace for the whole song. For the rest of the band's set they danced furiously and at the end

Spencer collapsed into a chair. Jessica, by contrast, was still jumping up and down until Tommy Coupland leapt from the stage and gathered her up in an embrace. A tall young man with a blond ponytail, Tommy was effusive in his praise, 'She taught me everything,' he said, grasping Spencer by the hand.

'Well, you know damn well that's not true,' laughed Jessica.

The three of them sat at the bar, where, full of post-performance adrenalin, Tommy shared his hopes and aspirations. At present, the band did not venture much out of the southern states, but there was talk of gigs in New York and a tour of California.

To his horror, Spencer saw a tall, grey-haired figure approaching. It was Bernard. He acknowledged Jessica and Spencer, then stretched out a hand to introduce himself to Tommy.

'I humbly thank you for an inspiring performance… as an aspiring practitioner of the art of the harmonica I wonder if you could enlighten me… '

Tommy's glazed look and fixed smile indicated that he was very familiar with people like Bernard.

'And of course,' simpered Bernard, 'we share a teacher, although I fear I may struggle to match your virtuosity, no matter how long I attend her classes.'

This assessment received no contradiction from Jessica.

'But I wonder,' Bernard continued, 'which particularly brand of instrument you favour?'

'Well I still like the Seydel, but nowadays I probably play a Crossover more than anything.'

'I personally play the Meisterklasse.' Bernard's smile was positively unctuous.

'Yep. Nice harp,' said Tommy, turning back towards Jessica.

Bernard was not to be shaken off quite so easily. 'And if I may trouble you for a moment longer... I would like to hear your view on the thorny question of 'breaking in' a harmonica. I know there is a school of thought that says a harp should not be played with volume or ...er... force until it has been gently 'broken in' for a matter of hours or even days...'

'It's bullshit. Nice to meet you. Goodbye.'

Dismissed, Bernard left.

Tommy told stories about life on the road with a blues band until finally Jessica had to make her apologies, 'I'm sorry, Tommy, but we need to get back.'

After midnight Spencer was driving back to Merganserville, with Jessica dozing in the passenger seat. He became aware of a white pick-up truck behind him. It sat on his tail for several miles. Spencer slowed right down and the pick-up slowed with him. He put his foot on the gas and the pick-up gained speed too, staying dangerously close. Eventually Spencer pulled over and the pick-up went past. It had Alabama plates.

Jessica woke as they were coming into town. 'Don't go through The Valley, Spencer, it's best avoided at this time of night.'

'Yes, I've been told.'

'There are some desperate people down there and you can get robbed at a stop-light.'

A few minutes later Spencer pulled over at Jessica's house.

'Spencer… do you have to work tomorrow?'

'Well, not till the afternoon.'

'Would you like to come in for a glass of wine?'

'That would be lovely.'

Glasses in hand, they talked about the gig, about music, about Pellier. They came to a pause. Jessica stroked the rim of her glass.

'Are you okay, Jessica?'

'I'm fine… really… I feel good. Spencer… would you like to stay tonight?'

'Do you mean...?'

'Yes, that's what I mean.'

'Well, er… are you sure?'

Jessica stood up, crossed the room and embraced him. She held him tightly in her arms, 'For God's sake say "Yes," before I change my mind.'

Spencer stayed with Jessica that night. And the next night. And the night after that.

CHAPTER EIGHT

'So what on earth are these? 'Marshmallow Mateys'? Good grief, I don't believe it,' Spencer called out from the kitchen.

'Marshmallow Mateys are a breakfast cereal. And your point is…?' Jessica was lying in bed.

'My point is… well, my first point is that there is probably more nutritional value in the cardboard box than there is in the Marshmallow Mateys themselves… '

'I happen to like them, and so does my nephew when he comes over to visit.'

'… And my second point is why do they sell something with such a puerile name? I wonder,' Spencer was warming to his theme, 'I wonder if you bought them in Piggly-Wiggly.'

'Possibly… '

'I mean it's this infantilism that runs through American life. Piggly-Wiggly? British people would just not go to a store with a name like that. It's the cult of the cute. In Britain, our great cultural icon is Shakespeare; in America it's Walt Disney.'

'Why don't you get your ass in gear and make me some coffee while you're ranting away? If I'd known you were such a cultural snob I would never have had sex with you. And I would like some of the 2 percent milk in the coffee, please. It's the one in the fridge with the picture of Donald Duck.'

'Really?'

'No! My God, you're not just a cultural snob – you're a gullible cultural snob. Let's get this straight: American 2 percent milk does *not* have a picture of Donald Duck, or Mickey Mouse, or Spiderman, or Charles Manson.'

Spencer smiled to himself, 'That's a shame. I would have bought the one with Charles Manson.'

He began to make breakfast, 'How do you like your eggs?'

'Unfertilised.'

'Ha bloody ha. Anyway, we took precautions.'

'Can I have two eggs, over easy?'

'Can I have a translation please?'

'Oh God, when are you people going to learn English?'

'And why is American bacon so dreadful?'

'I have no idea.'

'It's probably the way you slaughter them. You probably hunt them down on horseback and shoot them with Winchester rifles.'

'What do you do in England? Bore them to death?'

'We get the Danes to kill them for us. The Danes are our Canadians. Okay, look, I'll do you two fried eggs on rye toast, then I'll pour six pounds of sugar over it, and you'll have the average American breakfast.'

'All this from a nation that eats baked beans first thing in the morning. Anyway, if we eat so much sugar, why are you the ones with the bad teeth?'

'I shall treat that as the outdated stereotype that it is.'

After breakfast they sat on the porch. It was a warm morning with a gentle breeze.

'So… Spencer,' said Jessica, 'you'd be about 5ft 11?'

'5ft 11 inches exactly. How did you know?'

'Well, I know how tall I am, so it's pretty easy to estimate. But… would you weigh about 160… 170 pounds?'

'76 kilos.'

'Kilos? What voodoo is this?'

'It's the metric system. Heard of it?'

'I sure have. It's all part of a conspiracy to overthrow the American way of life and establish a New World Order.'

'Yep. You got it in one.'

'So what do you actually weigh?'

'12 stone.'

'12 stone? Cor Blimey Guv. How big are these stones? Pebbles? Paving stones?

'Okay. I'm 168 pounds.'

'Well, I was pretty close then. And your hair is… brown?'

'Mid-brown.'

'Mousy?'

'Anglo-Saxon.'

'Eyes?'

'Blue. Do you want my blood group… star sign?'

They sat in silence for a while. A feeling of contentment was warming Spencer's body. It was, for him, an unusual experience.

'You mentioned your nephew…' said Spencer.

'Yeah… I have a sister in Atlanta. She's married. Two children. I guess they come up here a couple of times a year. I'll go to be with them for Thanksgiving.'

'Close family?'

'No, not really. Not since Mama and Papa passed. Also… we didn't really grow up together, because I was off at the Blind School in Macon and then when I came back at vacations I was always competing with her, always trying to show that I was as good as her, even though I was blind. I was an ornery kid. I still am.'

For a while he looked at the way her hair curled on her shoulders.

'Jessica, I wanted to ask you something, and please forgive me if it's insensitive.'

'I'm sure I've heard worse. '

'If you can't see me… what attracted you to me?'

She smiled, as if to herself, 'Can you ever explain that, really? I mean, you're quite pompous and uptight because you're English, but you have a vulnerability that I find very sexy.'

'Oh, I see. Well… '

'It has a lot to do with the voice and the way that the personality comes through the voice. But it's intangible isn't it? I don't know…' She seemed distracted.

'So what was it that made you change your mind? About me, I mean.'

'I'm not sure that I did change my mind exactly… I think, I mean when you made a move on me I supposed I was just worried about what was attracting you to me, y'know? I don't know how to put this but… well, some white guys would be attracted by what they saw as the exotic and I really would find that demeaning.'

'Oh God, no, I would never… '

'Yes, I know, I can see that now, totally… look Spencer, I need some time to myself. I'm giving a lecture this afternoon and I need to run over it in my mind.'

'Sorry, I didn't realise you gave lectures.'

'Nearly all my teaching is in seminars, but, yes, I do give lectures, and I have one this afternoon… Sorry, I really need to get on with it.'

'Can I come and hear it?'

'Well I can't stop you. It's at 4 o'clock in the François de la Billière lecture hall.'

'What will you be talking about?'

'Post-Civil War Reconstruction. It's fairly general because it's intended for Freshmen and up.'

'Okay, I'll see you later.'

Jessica stood up with him and took him in her arms. 'See you later, sweetheart,' she breathed in his ear.

Spencer slid into his seat just before 4 o'clock. The hall was packed, and there was an expectant buzz in the air – far more so than he would have expected for an academic lecture. Jessica was greeted by loud applause, and even some shouts of approval. He was only just realising what a star of the campus she was. She spoke for forty-five minutes without notes, and without any kind of visual aid, and was utterly in command throughout. At the end, some of the students were stamping their feet. She took questions and dealt with even the most naïve enquiry with grace. Spencer thought she was just as much a performer here as when she was playing with her band. Even after it was all over, a crowd of students stood around her – it seemed as if they would never let her leave. Spencer slipped away. He felt outclassed as a teacher and outclassed as a person. He would have liked to have felt proud of her, but she had not granted him that right. Did he feel envious? Memories drifted back from his youth, memories of feeling unworthy of girls that he had pursued. Memories of (in their words) 'putting them on a pedestal'. He had outgrown all that, hadn't he?

****

Six in the evening had always been Spencer's cocktail hour. He hardly ever had a drink before then. At the appointed time, he found himself in Flanagan's with a beer in front of him. It was quiet at that time: there were seven or eight customers, all of them white men, all of them older than Spencer. He realised that he had never seen a black person in there.

Spencer had grown up in a white neighbourhood of an East Midland English town. At his secondary school there were a handful of Sikhs, but nobody from any other ethnic minority. He never thought of race. Then he went to university in the melting pot that is Birmingham, and he made friends with a number of black students. Again, he did not think of race as an issue and the subject never came up in conversation with his black friends. It was only later that he realised that it was, indeed, not an issue for him because he was part of the white majority.

People had talked to him about the Old South and the New South. They had described the slow transition from one to another. He wondered how he would be welcomed if he went into a black bar in Merganserville.

Spencer looked around the room. He liked bars early in the evening, before they grew crowded and noisy. He liked his thoughts to be accompanied by the quiet click of balls on the pool table. He exchanged pleasantries with Ted the bartender. Short, grey-haired and muscular, Ted was an old school barman: he was skilled at offering solace to the lost and the lonely, but equally capable of breaking up a fight. Did he keep a weapon behind the bar? Spencer drank his beer and pulled out his mobile phone. He sent photos of Merganserville to his children back home in London.

The door burst open and Lloyd stamped into the bar. He gave Spencer a cursory nod and called to the barman, 'Hey Ted, gimme a beer and a Jack.'

The barman poured a glass of draft beer and a shot of Jack Daniels. The whiskey went down in one gulp.

'Bad day at work, Lloyd?' ventured Spencer.

'Bad day… bad week… bad year.' He slid onto the stool next to Spencer's and spoke quietly. There was anger in his voice. 'What some of these bastards think they can get away with… I can't stand much more of it…' He looked at the basketball game on the TV at the end of the bar. 'The trouble is they're not actually interested in enforcing the law and protecting their community. They just want to cover up for their own kind. Anyway... fuck 'em.' He turned back to the game.

Late in the evening, Spencer stubbed out his cigarette on the porch and came into the apartment. Jessica was listening to a Jazz station coming out of Atlanta.

'Okay,' she said, 'You know the routine. Toothbrush, toothpaste, mouthwash and a dash of cologne.'

'I'll stick my head in a bucket of bleach if you like,' replied Spencer, moving towards the bathroom.

'When that becomes necessary, I'll let you know.'

'Do you know what I really think?' said Spencer, having completed the required ablutions. 'I think you don't really dislike the smell so much; all this is just to discourage me from smoking.'

'No shit, Sherlock. Don't you see that I have a vested interest in keeping you alive? And if you're fixing to take your shoes off, please put them up by the front door. I'm tired of tripping over them. Why are men so untidy?'

'This is like being married all over again. I thought you were just a floozy I could have a fling with, and you've turned into my ex-wife.'

'My house, my rules. You can smoke all you like in your own apartment.'

Spencer made himself comfortable on the sofa. Jessica closed her laptop and came to sit next to him. She moved with a grace that he found enchanting. She leant over to him and ran her fingers across his cheek.

'When are you going off to see your aunt… Miriam, is it?'

'Miriam, yes,' replied Spencer, 'I'll go on Saturday. I'll stay for Thanksgiving week. It'll give me a chance to look round Palm Springs. Will you miss me?'

'Sure I'll miss you.' Jessica was silent for a few moments, 'You're not actually married any more, are you Spencer?'

'No. My divorce came through some time ago. Why do you ask?'

'No reason.'

'Do you want me to make you some tea?'

'No thanks, sweetheart.'

They sat quietly for a while until Jessica spoke, 'You know Spencer, if you were wondering about it – my blindness is in no way genetic: it will not be passed on to any children I might have.'

'What's prompted that?'

'Nothing. Nothing at all.'

Spencer started to tell Jessica about his day at work when she suddenly interrupted.

'When your marriage broke up, was it just because of the gambling?'

'Well... there's never just one reason, but that's what sealed it. I had lied to her once too often, I suppose. I was an addict; I was in the grip of something... something that... I mean people understand alcoholism, but it's hard for them to understand addictive gambling. Most people don't see the point of it. The point of it, of course, is that it is the only addiction with a really tangible reward – you are rewarded with real money each time you win. It's like a loyalty card, and you don't get that with heroin.'

'Will you gamble again?'

'No. It's over. I'm sure of that. I have no need for it, no desire for it. It filled an emptiness within me, and I just don't feel that emptiness anymore.'

'So what filled it?'

'I don't know. Maybe the void is still there, but I'm just not conscious of it.'

He did not tell her what he really felt: that she had filled the emptiness more than anything else.

'I admire you, sweetheart. It's not easy to kick a habit like that.'

'Have you ever had an addiction, or compulsion, or whatever?'

'Well I've got a pretty serious Marshmallow Mateys habit.'

'I could have guessed that was coming...'

'I started out on Corn Flakes, but I soon moved on to the harder stuff... hahaha.'

'No, really… I mean if you don't mind me asking… have you ever had any of those sorts of issues?'

'I think some people have addictive personalities, and I'm just not like that.' She kissed him, 'I'm going to change into my night clothes.'

'Not those blue striped pyjamas I hope.'

'I'd say they were indigo rather than blue.'

It was amazing how often he forgot that she was blind.

'Sorry.'

'Why don't you like them anyway?'

'They're very unsexy.'

'Sorry, I forgot that women always have to dress to please men instead of keeping themselves warm and comfortable.'

'Here we go again… I'm England's answer to Hugh Hefner.'

'Hugh Hefner would have been the perfect husband: very rich and about to fall off his perch.'

Spencer watched Jessica undress. He spoke, 'Actually I'm always struck by how well you dress. You always look really elegant.'

'Thank you.'

'But how do you do it?'

'Do you really expect me to give away all my secrets?'

'Just curious.'

'Well, the truth is, a friend of mine usually comes over on Sunday and we choose my outfits for the week.'

'One of your girlfriends, presumably.'

'What if I were to tell you that it was a man?'

'If you were to tell me that I would be surprised.'

'Well it just so happens that it's Michael Donner who teaches Art History.'

'Oh, well, that's different.'

'What do you mean?'

'Well, he's gay, isn't he?'

'So?

'Gay men have good dress sense.'

'Oh my God, Spencer! Next you'll be telling me that Africans have a good sense of rhythm.'

'Well, look at all the top fashion designers – they're all gay men.'

'Well, actually they're not, but…'

'I've always thought that was a bit strange…'

'I've always thought you were a bit strange…'

'No, but look,' said Spencer, 'it doesn't really make sense that women's clothes are designed by men who do not desire women.'

'So you think women's clothes should be designed by straight men?'

'It seems logical.'

'So, if you were designing women's clothes, what would you come up with?'

'Obviously, it would depend on the woman… if I were designing for you, for example, well… I would let my imagination run wild. Four-inch heels, of course, and then should we go for a thong or maybe forget underwear altogether… '

'Well... talk about sleeping with the enemy.'

Spencer was quiet for a moment. 'I was wondering when that phrase would come up.'

'I was joking. You do know when I'm joking, don't you?'

'Yes, but… I mean… I'm a white man, and I could be seen as part of the oppressor group, and I have sometimes wondered what your friends have said. I mean, the black women particularly.'

'Well, look Spencer, darling, I will be absolutely honest with you. Some of my friends have expressed surprise that I'm dating you.'

'And is that because of race, or feminism, or what?'

'No… no, nothing like that. They just can't understand why I'm screwing an ugly-looking fucker like you. But I just tell them I'm blind so it doesn't matter.' Jessica buttoned up her pyjamas and picked up her headphones.

Spencer started to get ready for bed. 'What's your bedtime listening at the moment?' he asked.

'*Wuthering Heights.*'

'Oh… who's reading it?'

'Johnny Cash.'

'*Johnny Cash*? Really?'

Jessica cracked up, 'No, of course it isn't Johnny fucking Cash, you idiot! It's dramatised. There are several voices. It's good. It works well.'

'Have you heard it before?'

'Many times. I read it in Braille when I was aged fourteen, and I wanted to go to bed with Heathcliff even then.'

'Well, that's exactly what you're doing.'

'Until someone better comes along, Spencer.'

'Is Heathcliff black?'

'I'll call Emily Bronte: I've got her on speed-dial.'

'You know what I mean. Does he represent the Outsider, the Other, in a way that a black man would have done at that time?'

'I'm a historian, not a literary critic. Anyway, I don't read that book for its depiction of an inter-racial relationship. That's not what it's about, is it?'

Spencer sat for a moment in silence.

'Jessica, can I ask you something? Have any of your other boyfriends been white?'

'How would I know?' replied Jessica, giggling.

'Okay, look, I know it may not matter to you, and I know it doesn't matter to me, but here in Georgia it matters to some people a hell of a lot.'

Jessica sighed, 'Spencer, I am constantly going out on a limb so that I can live my life the way I want to live it. Do you really think I would let other people's prejudice stop me from going to bed with a white man? Now, can I get back to Heathcliff?'

In the small dark hours of the night, Spencer drifted out of sleep. Beside him, Jessica slept on. He let his eyes adjust to the semi-darkness of the room and then looked at her face for a long time. He almost felt ashamed that his emotions could still catch him out. He was forty-one years old. He had been through a marriage; he had watched two children growing up. He had fought his way out of an addiction. What was there left to surprise him? Surely there were only a certain number of new emotions available to him – he'd already had a chance to run through the gamut of feelings that a human being was heir to, so what could be left? He remembered when his first child was born, how he felt that he had found all the love he could find within himself. How could he find more? But then his son was born and he found more love – more than he had thought possible. Somehow, inexplicably, it was happening again. Somehow, Jessica was breaking the rules, reinventing the form. It was the first time he had felt anything like this for many years.

Sex is such a strange thing, he thought. In Western countries we are surrounded by it almost all the time, and yet one has so little idea of what other people get up to behind closed doors. He and his male friends never discussed their sexual encounters in any detail. It was like playing the world's most popular game without ever being taught the rules.

He remembered his first kiss at fourteen, his first fumbling attempt at sex at seventeen. He thought back to falling in love with Sarah and remaining in love with her through their marriage and their break-up, and still being in love with her till… till when? Till the moment he met Jessica?

The woman beside him stirred in her sleep, muttered something and settled.

With every other woman he had known, sex had been generally enjoyable and sometimes thrilling – but it had always been desperately serious. Jessica somehow took the tension out of the situation. He was daring with her, but never sombre. What he did with her could be highly erotic and terribly funny at the same time. He sometimes thought he was playing the straight man in a carnal double act.

He checked the clock beside the bed. It was 5am. He knew he would not return to sleep. He eased himself out of bed and walked to the bathroom. There was a full-length mirror on one of the walls. He assumed this was for friends and house-guests, since Jessica would surely have little use for it herself. He stared at himself, naked, for a long time. He had never liked his body very much; he had never felt proud of the way he looked. He knew that he had never been the kind of man to turn women's heads in the street. Was he attracted to a blind woman precisely because she would not care what he looked like? Was that even true? Did Jessica not want her man to be admired by other women for his looks? That was natural, wasn't it? But was he 'her man' anyway? He had never said that she was 'his woman'.

Spencer had fallen in love. Did Jessica feel the same way?

****

On Tuesday morning Spencer finished his seminar and met Jessica for lunch.

'How was it?' she asked him.

'Not good. We didn't really get anywhere today.'

'Which play were you talking about?'

'Well, that's just it. It was *Twelfth Night* – the most non-binary play of the lot. All the gender-bending we have today… Shakespeare got there first. But still this bunch don't see its relevance. You'd think Mark maybe would have something to say but no… he just sat there in his Marlon Bloody Brando T-shirt and said nothing.'

They both ordered salad. Here in Georgia Spencer knew that even a salad would have enough calories for a bus-load of sumo wrestlers.

'In *Twelfth Night*,' he continued, 'people fall in love with Viola thinking she's a woman, and other people fall in love with her thinking she's a man. The point is… they fall in love with a *person*, an *individual*, not a binary label, and not because she belongs to any particular group. Also, of course, it's one of several examples in Shakespeare where someone gains a degree of freedom through cross-dressing. I would have thought these students could relate to that. But they don't. Maybe it's me. Maybe another teacher would handle this situation better than I do.' He chewed a lettuce leaf. 'I've set them their written work. God knows what they'll come up with.'

'What's the assignment?'

'They have to write a comparison between two of the plays we've studied. They have to write about the themes and how those themes could be realised in performance. I'm grading them on it, and I have to be fair, but I know I'll get the party line. Shakespeare is 'Pale, Stale and Male'. It's amazing how quickly a bold and adventurous idea becomes a liberal platitude. Not so much liberal, actually, more Stalinist. Don't go against the orthodox way of thinking. It's as if identity politics has stopped them understanding what an individual is. I mean, theatre is about empathy: you put yourself in someone else's shoes.

That seems to me to get lost. One of them said today that a gay character has to be played by a gay actor. What's all that about? Talk about the death of the imagination.'

'You know Spencer, you're starting to sound like one of those Angry White Men railing against Political Correctness.'

'Great. I can get a job with Fox News. I'm sure you know that's not where I'm coming from.'

'Yes, but people organise in groups according to race, gender, sexuality etc. for good reason, and often with good results. Social change is achieved by groups, by communities of interest, you might say. I can choose to be a member of three groups who are fighting to effect change – women, black people and the blind. You see how lucky I am?'

Spencer gave his silent smile: the one he used when he wasn't sure if she was joking.

'Jessica, look… I feel what I feel for you not because you're a member of a group but because you're you. That's the most important thing of all.'

'You have the luxury of saying that because you are a white man.'

Spencer toyed with his salad.

'I mean I think I understand what you're saying,' he said, 'but where is the individual in all of this?'

'The individual is the beating heart of the group – I don't see a problem. Don't you have these debates back home?'

'Not to the same extent. Well, not where *I* work, anyway.'

Jessica took a drink of water. 'I understand what you say about empathy, but surely there are limits. I mean, just as an example …could a sighted white man write a novel about a blind black woman?'

'I don't know. I've never thought about it.'

'Well,' said Jessica, 'I think he'd be a fool to try.'

CHAPTER NINE

The screen on Spencer's mobile lit up with Jessica's number. He pulled the Mustang over to the kerb and answered.

'Hello sweetheart. I just wanted to know if you arrived safely.'

'Yes, I'm fine. Sorry – I was going to call you as soon as I got to Miriam's.'

'You've rented a car?'

'Yes. It took a while because Palm Springs airport was jammed with people.'

'Yeah, well. I said it would be busy in Thanksgiving Week. But you got a car okay?'

'I got a Mustang. It's red. It's fantastic.'

'And what did that cost?'

'Not much. More than a Nissan, but well… you know… this is California.'

'You really are an idiot, Spencer.'

'But I saved money by not renting a GPS.'

'Where are you now?'

'I'm not sure. Somewhere in the Palm Springs area.'

'So, let's get this straight – you rented a Mustang, but you didn't get GPS so you could save money – and now you're lost?'

'I'm not lost – I'm just coming to terms with a new environment. I'll sort it out. I know that Aunt Miriam lives at Lake View Creek. From the airport I drove onto Gene Autry Trail, then hung a left on Dinah Shore Drive, then right on Bob Hope Drive, left on Gerald Ford Drive, and that's when I went wrong. I turned right into Frank Sinatra Drive… '

'When you should have turned onto Dean Martin Boulevard, left on Frankie Valli Crescent, under Fred Astaire Bridge and onto Ginger Rogers Road… '

'There actually is a Ginger Rogers Road.'

'You're kidding!'

'At the airport there's a concourse named after Sonny Bono. I don't know why, but that just would not give me confidence if I were about to get on a plane.'

'Apparently,' said Jessica, 'in Mongolia there is an airport called Moron.'

Spencer laughed. 'Who flies there? Virgin?'

'What's wrong with Virgin?'

'Who wants to travel with something that doesn't go all the way?'

'Don't give up the day job.'

'I'll call you when I get to my Aunt Miriam's place.'

Spencer had assumed that Aunt Miriam's house would be easy to find because she lived in a gated community. He had not realised that in Palm Springs every community is a gated community. Where did the poor people live? Perhaps they commuted from Mexico.

At last Spencer found himself in the living-room of Aunt Miriam's small, but well-appointed, apartment. Aunt Miriam, a trim seventy, sleek in a pants suit, poured tea for Spencer and herself and for the four men who had joined them. Dwayne and Harry were about forty; Bobby and Jack a little older. Spencer was struck by how well-groomed and neatly dressed the men were. Ralph Lauren was holding his own.

'We've heard so much about you, Spencer,' offered Harry.

'All good I hope,' Spencer replied.

'Oh, we preferred the bad parts,' said Jack to chuckles all round.

'We're having a party at our place tonight and we would love it if you could come,' said Harry.

'Well, I would like that,' said Spencer, after an almost undetectably brief hesitation.

'We'll pick you up at eight. We're only two blocks away, but nobody walks anywhere in Palm Springs.'

'Okay. See you later.'

After a brief nap, Spencer joined Miriam for cocktails.

'This party tonight… I take it there won't be any women there?'

'I think that's a fair bet. Are you okay with that? Actually, Spencer, I think you could pass for gay. If it weren't for those shoes.'

Spencer glanced down at his sensible and competitively-priced footwear.

She continued, 'I've met so many of these gay boys since I've been here, and they've been so kind to me, I can't tell you.'

'Well, I don't mind going, as long as I don't have to listen to a lot of Judy Garland records.'

'That's just a tiny bit old-fashioned of you, isn't it Spencer?'

'Will I have anything in common with a bunch of gay men?'

'Why not, for heaven's sake?'

'Well, it's not just a question of sexuality is it? There's a gay sensibility. It's a whole different way of seeing the world. At my university I have to be aware of something called Queer Theory, and that's all about…'

'Spencer,' interrupted Miriam, 'you're going to a party, not a seminar on Michel Foucault.'

Spencer stared at Miriam. Miriam looked pleased with herself.

He took a moment to recover, 'Well, I don't really think it will be my kind of thing. Don't wait up, but I think I'll be back before eleven.'

It was at 6am that Dwayne and Harry deposited a semi-comatose Spencer back at Miriam's apartment, tactfully divested him of his outer clothing and safely tucked him up in bed. He woke at noon, and gradually the events of the previous evening crept upon him.

His memory of the earlier part of the evening was fairly clear. There had been only five or six guys there when he arrived, and he was surprised to find himself sitting, cocktail in hand, watching a TV show called 'Queer Eye for the Straight Guy'. He did not see much entertainment value in observing an awkward man in his thirties having a haircut and a cookery lesson, and then trying on various outfits, but the rest of the group seemed to enjoy it immensely. As the house filled up and the volume-level rose he was even more surprised to see an Ariana Grande concert playing on the TV. He could completely understand why heterosexual men might enjoy watching Ariana Grande, but why on earth should she interest gay men? None of it was making any sense. He had several more cocktails and several diverting conversations, and around 11pm he was offered a spliff. It was described as 'high-grade stuff'. It was about this time that the dancing began, and Spencer decided it was a good idea to throw some moves. After midnight… he was hazy on what had happened after midnight. Just not hazy enough… As Spencer lay in bed, more details began to worm their way into his memory.

'Oh no, did I really do that… oh my God.'

Then he remembered that he had promised to go for lunch with Bobby and Jack. He had, in fact, suggested it. He had, in fact, offered to pay. He looked at the clock and scrambled for the shower.

Spencer sat with Bobby and Jack at the Armadillo. They sat on a terrace swathed with vine leaves in the dry desert warmth. It was refreshing after the humidity of Georgia. After a little banter with the cute young waiter, lunch was ordered. Spencer looked about him. There were gay couples at almost every table, nearly all of them older than Bobby and Jack. There were some people well into their seventies. Spencer had always felt that London was a young person's town: older people – particularly poorer older people – looked defensive, hunted. The people around him here seemed comfortable in their skin, comfortable with each other and with the environment, and they were not, of course, poor.

There were a few jokes about Spencer's behaviour at the party, but he was able to wrestle the conversation away to a discussion on life in Palm Springs. Bobby and Jack had lived there for five years and saw no reason to live anywhere else.

'How long have you two been together?' asked Spencer.

The two men smiled at each other. 'It's coming up to twenty-five years,' said Bobby.

'We both grew up in Fargo, in North Dakota, and we met when we were freshmen at North Dakota State. Things were… well, let's just say things were not so good for gay people in North Dakota… not back then anyway.'

'I don't think it's changed much,' said Jack.

'Gay people were invisible,' said Bobby. 'It was dreadful. You had to hide who you were. You lived in fear, y'know? Fear of discovery. So eventually we moved to San Francisco where we could be ourselves at last. And then finally we came here.'

'Do you have a partner in London, Spencer?' asked Jack.

'No. My marriage came to an end nearly four years ago, and there hasn't really been anyone since. Except…' he paused, not sure of what to say, 'well, I've met someone here in the States and… well, I think I'm in love.'

Bobby and Jack looked both intrigued and delighted. Spencer spilled the beans, telling them how he had met Jessica, how the relationship had developed, and how he felt about her. As an afterthought he mentioned that she was black. Bobby and Jack talked about their own experiences of inter-racial relationships, which turned out to be very limited indeed.

It was only when he arrived back at Miriam's that Spencer realised that he had not mentioned that Jessica was blind.

The following day he took Miriam out in his rented Mustang to the Joshua Tree National Park. On the way, she talked about her life. He had never spent much time with her, and most of it was new to him. She had exchanged Kettering for California in the late 1960s, and had had a wild time of it as a young woman in Los Angeles. Jobs were easy to find, and after her marriage in 1971 to an advertising executive called Ryan Donohue she continued to work, although she did not really need to. She had always been an independently minded woman, more so, perhaps, than her sister Joan, who gave up work as soon as Spencer was born in 1976. Miriam had, essentially, enjoyed a happy marriage and a fulfilling life until Ryan's death five years earlier.

'I was heartbroken, just devastated, when Ryan died,' said Miriam, as they drove along Highway 62. 'That's when I moved out to Palm Springs and it turned out to be the right decision. I have a new life now.' She gazed out at a sunny California morning. 'Don't get me wrong… the pain does not go away… but I don't feel so empty now. When it first happened, I don't know, there seemed to be no point to anything, and… well, I don't feel that now. I've made new friends. I'm involved in charity work. I try to help others… God knows there are so many people worse off than me.'

They arrived at the entrance to the National Park. There was a primitive beauty about the desert landscape and the spiky, twisted trees. Mormon settlers gave the name to the iconic tree because it made them think of Joshua holding up his hands in prayer. But were the trees reaching up to touch God, or were they reaching up to pull the sky down upon them?

Spencer pulled over to watch a coyote looking for road-kill.

'Miriam, I would really like it if you could tell me a little about the family, because I really never asked my parents much and now they're gone. I mean I remember my Gran, your mother, er… it was Esther, wasn't it?'

'Yes, she would have been born about 1926, and I think lived her whole life in the East Midlands. She married my father when she was nineteen or twenty, so your mother and I grew up in Kettering, and then Dad died when we were teenagers. Looking back on it, I think that spurred me on to grab hold of life and go to Los Angeles. I didn't feel there was much to grab hold of in Kettering.'

'You could have tried Northampton,' laughed Spencer.

'But that's just it, isn't it? I'm sure there are many people who would swap their lives in LA for a quiet little town in England.'

'Oh, I knew from an early age that I wanted to live in the big city. So I went to university in Birmingham, and then I was off to London as soon as possible. I don't regret it. I mean, things went wrong for me eventually… with my marriage breaking up and everything, but I know I would not have been happy just living my life in my home town.'

He watched the coyote leave the road and disappear behind a clump of rocks.

'So, Miriam, my grandmother was Esther. What about her mother?'

'Yes, that's when it gets interesting. Your maternal grandmother was called Sarah, and she was born Poland in about 1900. She came to Britain in the very early 1920s.'

'From Poland?'

'Yes, of course. Didn't you know that?'

'But her name was Miller.'

'Well, it was all about assimilation then, wasn't it? They changed it to Miller from Manischewitz. Did you really not know that?'

'I had no idea… but I didn't talk to my mother about her family.' He paused, as the implications began to dawn on him, 'My maternal grandmother came from Poland and was called Sarah Manischewitz?'

'I can't believe nobody told you all this. Maybe by the time you were born none of it seemed important anymore.'

'So they were… Jews?'

'Yes, of course, they were. And as you may know, a person's Jewishness runs through the maternal line, so…'

'So?'

'So you're a Jew, Spencer.'

Spencer and Miriam watched the sunset and then began to drive back through the National Park. As it grew dark, Spencer realised that his aunt had fallen asleep. He stopped the car and walked a little way from the road. He looked at the dark lunar landscape around him. The desert was silent, eternal. The Serrano, the Chemehuevi, and the Cahuilla tribes had all lived there, and had all passed on. Even the white man had made little lasting mark here. He looked up at the billion stars above him. His own life, his own particular contribution, seemed very small and insignificant. After his death, how would he be remembered? And for how long? He was not even an important part of his children's lives, so would they think of him after he had gone?

It was cold. Spencer walked back to the car.

Sometimes, thought Spencer, as he took his seat on the plane, the fates are with us. The man sitting next to him was wearing a *yarmulke*. Spencer introduced himself and they talked non-stop till they changed planes at Phoenix. He was called Daniel Wolf and he had a legal practice in Scottsdale, Arizona. He was highly amused to hear that Spencer had just joined the ranks of Jewry.

'I think it would depend on the rabbi you spoke to, but some would say that, yes, you are Jewish and that you could emigrate to Israel.'

'I'm not sure that I really want to do that.'

'Have you been?'

'No, never.'

'Obviously Israelis have every reason to feel defensive, but they are not easy people to get on with. They say an Israeli can start a fight in an empty house.' Daniel chuckled to himself. 'The thing is, you are not Jewish in any meaningful sense because you have not grown up in Jewish culture. Technically though – yes, you are Jewish.'

'Jewish enough for Hitler?'

'Ouch! Yes.'

'Do you go to synagogue?'

'Yes, I have to go. I can't explain it, but I have to go.'

'What are the basic tenets of your faith?'

'Oh, good grief – we'd need a flight to New York to have time for that.' Daniel thought for a moment. 'There is one particular concept that means a great deal to me.'

Spencer leaned in.

'In Hebrew, it is 'Tikkun Olam'. It means 'Repair the World'. Social justice is crucial to Judaism, and the individual is obliged to act for the common good.'

'"Repair the World". Yes… but what if the world can't be repaired?'

'There is always hope… always.' Daniel gazed out of the window for a while, then spoke, 'It's odd that your family never talked about their Jewish history. Do you think it was a fear of anti-Semitism at the time that caused the discussion to be closed?'

'Maybe,' said Spencer, 'it doesn't go away, does it? Living here in America, do you ever feel unsafe?'

'Well, as a Jew in Arizona I feel conspicuous, certainly. And then in places like Wyoming and Idaho, Jews are as rare as hen's teeth.'

The captain announced their descent into Phoenix.

'Actually, you know, Spencer, I don't think you are a Jew.'

'Aren't I?'

'No. As my father used to say, 'You are not a Jew unless you have fear in the marrow of your bones', and I don't think you have that. Or do you?'

****

It was Friday evening at Jessica's house. After dinner they were sitting together, drinking wine and listening to Nina Simone.

'Have you quit smoking,' asked Jessica, 'because I can't smell it on you.'

'Well, I had a cigarette at home two hours ago.'

'Oh. Well, that's a disappointment.'

'I put the butt in a sealed lead container and buried it 300 feet underground. Then I soaked my clothes in sulphuric acid, exfoliated my entire body and burnt my shoes.'

'So you *have* quit.'

'Yes, as of a week ago. I couldn't find anywhere to smoke in California, so that sealed it. Marijuana is legal there now, but tobacco is the work of the devil.'

'Well I think it's wonderful that you've quit. Stick with it.'

They sat without speaking for a while. Jessica broke the silence.

'Can you tell me anything else about Palm Springs?

'Well, no… I think I've told you everything.'

'Well, I can tell there's something on your mind, so do you want to tell me about it?'

'Well, it's nothing really.'

'Did something else happen? Apart from finding out that you were one of the Chosen People, which I can see will have come as something of a surprise. I mean, next week you might find out that you're a Hindu as well.'

'Who's being flippant now? I really don't think you should joke about it. You know as well as I do that millions of people died because of their Jewish identity. It's a very serious matter and it should not be trivialised.'

'My God, are all English men as pompous as you are?'

'Most of them. Especially the Jews.'

'Yes, well… we had our holocaust too, you know.'

'Why don't you tell me something I don't know?'

'People talk about Auschwitz all the time, but they never talk about the Middle Passage. It's a fact that millions of Africans died being transported from Africa to America, and the ones who didn't die spent the rest of their lives in slavery, with white people seeing the profits.'

'Yes, I know… I know.' said Spencer, 'I am fully aware of all that, but there is nothing I can do about it now. Do you want me to feel guilty about it?'

Jessica groaned, 'You see, I get that all the time… white people saying that, as if there is no such thing as collective guilt. The fact is you still profit from the legacy of slavery. I don't think it's useful for you to feel guilty about it, but I do want you to at least be aware of it.'

He was quiet for a moment. 'Can I just say… Auschwitz is in living memory and slavery really isn't.'

'So it's just a question of the passage of time?' said Jessica

'Yes, partly…'

'Anyway, we've established that you are now part of a cabal that is conspiring to take over the world.'

Spencer chuckled to himself, 'That's about the size of it.'

'How's that going, by the way?'

'Not too well at the moment.'

They sat together for a long time. Jessica drank some wine. Finally she spoke.

'So, are you going to tell me what's on your mind?'

'Well, I don't know how to say it.'

There was a long pause.

'I told you that my aunt Miriam has lots of gay friends?'

'Yes, and…?'

'Well, there was a party… '

'Yes, and…?'

'Well, we had a lot to drink… '

'Yes, and…?'

'Well… I kind of got into a clinch with a guy called Ronald'

'A "clinch"… and then what happened?'

'Well… I kind of let him kiss me.'

'And?'

'Well… I kind of liked it.'

Jessica stood and turned away from him. She spoke very softly, 'How could you do such a thing?'

'Oh God, I'm sorry. Look, I shouldn't have mentioned it; I'm sorry.' He stood and tentatively held her shoulders from behind. Her shoulders were shaking. 'Wait a minute,' said Spencer, 'are you laughing?'

Jessica doubled up with uncontrollable glee. 'How do you do it? I mean, how the fuck do you do it?' She was on her knees, sobbing with mirth. Eventually she spoke, 'Only you, you idiot, only you could have your first gay encounter with someone called Ronald!'

'You don't mind then?'

'Well, if he'd fucked your tail, I really would have had something to say about it, but I take it that didn't happen?'

'No it most certainly did not.'

'I guess I can live with a kiss, but don't do it again, okay?'

'I'm not planning to attend any more gay parties.'

'Well, Mr Uptight Limey, it may interest you to know that my first lover was a woman, and an older woman at that.'

'*What*?'

'Do you actually think it's unusual? I was in my Freshman year at college, and I met a postgrad student called Jeanette. I went to bed with her three times. Then I realised that I wasn't really gay, and I met my first boyfriend soon after that.'

'So, you were, what, eighteen?'

'Yeah, I was eighteen. Jeanette was lovely. She was actually gorgeous in bed because a woman knows another woman's body. Most men need a road map.'

'Oh, I see.' Spencer paused for a moment, 'Do I need a road map?'

'You need GPS most of the time, you Limey bastard.' She left him and went into the kitchen. Spencer sipped his wine.

Jessica returned with a large pair of scissors in her hand.

'Right, so if you're Jewish you won't be needing that bit of skin on the end of your cock. Let's sort that out now…'

'Well that just shows how little you know about it. If you convert to Judaism, you don't have to be circumcised – you can have a symbolic prick instead.'

Jessica's giggles were taking over again, 'A *what*? A "symbolic prick"? Well when you've had a drink that's all your prick is to me anyway. Actually, not symbolic so much as virtual… I've made up my mind: you've got to have it done or you're a goddamn hypocrite. Nearly all my boyfriends have been cut anyway, and I think I prefer it.'

'Well that's because you're a barbarian like most Americans. We're a little more civilised and sophisticated in Europe.'

Jessica was snipping at the air malevolently as she approached, 'No… we've got to get it out of the way right now. No blow-jobs for you until you're cut.'

'If I intended to be circumcised, and I do not, I don't think I would choose to have the act performed by a woman with no medical qualifications who also just happened to be rather drunk and … er… blind.'

'Oh, I can see what's really going on here … this is about race isn't it? If I were a white woman who was medically unqualified, drunk and blind, well that would be okay wouldn't it?'

'Well, yes, obviously…'

Jessica placed the scissors on the coffee table and slid across the sofa towards Spencer. 'How is that "symbolic prick" getting on?' she murmured.

CHAPTER TEN

'Why don't I drive you up there in my car and the band can travel in the van? That way, if you want to get away straight after the gig, you won't have to wait for them to pack the equipment away.'

'Well, that sounds great, sweetheart, if you don't mind. We have to go up early for the sound check so you'll have to hang around for a while before we start...'

'That's okay. How far is it?'

'About twenty miles. It's a bar on the edge of a small town called Greensburg. We've played there before.'

'Fine. I'll pick you up at six.'

They were driving out of Merganserville in the early evening when Jessica spoke.

'You know Walt Hite, don't you?'

'Yes, I've spent some time with Walt. He's been good to me.'

Jessica was silent.

'What about Walt anyway? Why did you mention him?'

'Look, this is really unfair and I probably shouldn't mention it, because the matter was dealt with at the time, but... '

'Yes?'

Jessica sighed, 'About six months ago a student called Marie Smith made an allegation that he had sexually assaulted her. There was an investigation but the student dropped the case almost immediately.'

'Sexual assault?'

'Yes. Walt took her to the movies and kissed her in his car at the end of the evening. He said that it was just a kiss and that the student did not object. Marie told the student counselling service that it was much more than a kiss, and that she did not consent to it. Then she withdrew the allegation. Someone in the student counselling service told me that Marie was falling apart and could not face going through an enquiry.'

'My God! I can't imagine it. I mean, of course, you can never tell but Walt... I mean he doesn't seem the type.'

'I don't think there is a "type".'

'But the matter was dropped?'

'Yes,' said Jessica, 'I mean, it was pointed out to Walt Hite that taking a female student to the movies was not appropriate behaviour, but that was the end of it. The trouble is…'

'What?'

'The trouble is that I am teaching Marie now, and she has told me that Walt has been calling her and making sexual suggestions and God knows what, and that she is finding it all really upsetting.'

'That's *appalling*! I mean, if it's true, it's *appalling*.'

'I have to report it to the University authorities. I have no choice. But you should just stay out of it.'

'Well, yeah, I mean I won't mention it…'

The light was fading as they arrived in Greensburg. Monty's Music Lounge was one of the more significant buildings in a town that was not so much sleepy as comatose.

It was a one-horse town and the horse had left. Monty's stood at the end of a line of houses on the road heading out to the north. The band arrived and Spencer helped them unload their instruments and equipment. During the sound check Spencer stepped outside. He stood in darkness by the side of the club and stared up at the night sky. He was just picking out the familiar constellations when he heard a footfall behind him. He turned too late. His arms were grabbed and pinned behind his back. A sack went over his head. He felt the blade of a knife at his throat. There was a voice in his ear. The voice was dry and scaly like a lizard.

'We're gonna cut you some slack 'cause you don't really understand how things work here. We ain't even gonna hurt you; we're just giving you a warning. You just carry on teaching your Shakespeare, and stay away from nigger protest marches and stay away from that blind nigger bitch. She's causing trouble for us – don't let her cause trouble for you. Okay?'

The knife was removed from his neck. A sudden impact in the small of his back sent him sprawling. On the ground, he heard the two men running away. Carefully he brought himself to his feet and pulled the sack from his head. He went back into the bar and cleaned up in the rest room. When he came out the bar was filling up. He poked his head round the door of the dressing room.

'Have a good gig you guys.'

'Are you okay sweetheart?'

'Yes I'm fine. Everything's fine.'

At midnight Spencer and Jessica lay in bed.

'Spencer...?'

'Yes my darling, what is it?'

'I just… I wonder if you've actually thought about the implications… I mean, if we're going to be an item?'

Spencer thought for a moment. If he were to mention now that he had been threatened before the gig, how would she react? He did not want to terrify her, but it also felt wrong that he was trying to protect her from things she understood better than he did. He fumbled for the words.

'I know I come from a different culture and I know I didn't really understand that at first, but the whole race thing just doesn't matter for me…'

'No, I didn't mean that. I meant have you really thought about what it will be like to be with a blind woman?'

'I've thought about it, yes, but it's all new for me, and I suppose I'm on a learning curve, but we seem to be doing okay.'

He ran his hands across her body, 'All I know for sure is that I wanted you the moment I met you, and I haven't felt this way for a very long time.'

She kissed him.

'I know,' said Spencer, 'that it was not like that for you.'

Jessica chuckled, 'How can it be love at first sight when you can't see?'

They were silent for a long time.

'Spencer…?'

'Yes?'

She did not reply.

'What is it, Jessica? Is something wrong?'

'No… it's nothing, really.'

'Tell me.'

There was a long pause. She extended a hand. He took it. In the dim light he could see that she was crying.

'Er… you see, Spencer, I've never felt this about a man before. I would actually really like to know what you look like.'

Spencer held her hand. He never wanted to let it go.

****

On Tuesday morning Spencer examined the breakfast menu in Loretta's Luncheonette and wondered why so many American dishes could be made to sound so unattractive: 'Dirty Fried Eggs', 'Grits', 'Sausage Gravy'. Then there were the dishes that were designed to keep doctors in funds: the pastries the size of planets, the gravity-defying stacks of pancakes drowning in maple syrup. Spencer felt virtuous with his omelette and iced water.

'So did you get to play golf?' It was Walt, sliding into the seat opposite.

'There are 124 golf courses in Palm Springs and I avoided all of them,' said Spencer.

'So what *did* you do?'

'Oh, you know, hung out…' It was all too complicated to explain.

Walt ordered coffee.

'I'm having a poker game this week. Would you like to come?'

'Oh, well, look Walt, er… you know I had a gambling problem.'

'This is different. This is a friendly game for very small stakes, and it'll be a chance for you to meet a few normal guys who don't teach in universities, and don't talk about Proust and Nietzsche and all that bullshit.'

'I really don't know… '

'Think about it, okay?'

Spencer walked over to the rehearsal rooms. He was meant to have an input into the student productions of Shakespeare on campus so he watched a full dress rehearsal of *The Merchant of Venice*. It was being directed by a post-graduate student called Melissa Francome and Dani was playing Portia.

Rehearsal Studio 1 was large enough to accommodate an invited audience, and Spencer took his seat with twenty other people, most of them students, with a few academics dotted about. The play was performed without a set, with a minimum of props and with the actors dressed in simple rehearsal clothes. The original text had been heavily cut, and some new scenes had been added, notably gay sex scenes between Antonio and Bassanio and between Portia and Nerissa. Shylock's scenes had been cut more than most, to the extent that he hardly appeared in the play. In a question and answer session afterwards, Melissa Francome explained that she had seen her role as a liberator of Shakespeare from the heterosexist prison to which he, a fundamentally Queer playwright, had been confined. Spencer's head was starting to swim.

'I have a question,' he said.

'Yes, Doctor Leyton,' replied Melissa Francome.

'Why do you describe Shakespeare as a Queer playwright?'

'Well… I would have thought that was obvious.'

'It is not obvious to me.'

Other members of the small audience shifted in their seats.

'Well,' continued Melissa, 'much of his work is an exploration of non-binary character…'

'Do you mean that he rejected labels and anything else that restricts human potential? Good. I think we are starting to find common ground.'

'I think you know perfectly well, Doctor Leyton, that I am not saying that at all. Would you acknowledge that a classic play is a play that can be reinvented for every age, and that in fact that is what makes it a classic?'

'Yes, I certainly would agree with that, and honestly I admire attempts to break new ground. I mean every approach has validity, but does this serve Shakespeare? Surely there is a difference between reinvention and distortion?'

'*Distortion*?' There was anger in Melissa's voice. 'I take it that you are not going to deny that Shakespeare was gay in his personal life?'

'Actually I think I am denying it. The concept would have meant nothing to him. The Elizabethans did not define themselves by their sexuality. A man might have sex with men, women and farmyard animals, but it only defined what he did – not who he was. They just did not think in those terms. Okay, look, I know this is not the first production of this play to find a homoerotic element in the relationship between Antonio and Bassanio, but… I mean, for God's sake, what is gained by a Sapphic tryst between Portia and Nerissa?'

'*A Sapphic tryst*?' Melissa Francome looked primed to explode.

'There is no justification in the text and it just looks ridiculous. Quite apart from anything else, it requires a deep level of commitment from the performers and student actors are not up to it. They do not have the experience.'

Horrified glances were being exchanged amongst the students in the audience.

'Do I have to remind you, Doctor Leyton, that Shakespeare wrote half of his sonnets – a series of passionate love poems – to a man?'

'He also wrote in the voice of a man who wants to kill the king of Scotland, but that does not make him a regicide. The point is that it doesn't matter. Okay, look, I totally get it that we are still reacting against centuries of criticism that could not countenance the possibility of a gay Shakespeare, but right now it's swinging too far in the other direction. It's not important whether or not Shakespeare was gay, or a woman, or a Catholic, or a Freemason, or any of the other things that have been suggested. All that matters is his genius.'

There was a pause. Melissa looked at Spencer as if he were something she had found on the bottom of her shoe.

'Well, thank you for your contribution,' she smiled through thin lips. 'It's always refreshing to hear the traditional view.'

'Thank you. I haven't finished. And it is *not* the traditional view. Which tradition, for god's sake?' Spencer took a deep breath, 'Why have you cut Shylock out of the play?'

'Because unfortunately, in keeping with the prejudices of his time, Shakespeare depicted Shylock as a monster. It is an anti-Semitic portrait.'

'No. The play is a *critique* of anti-Semitism, and a highly prophetic one. He is showing us that if people are treated with inhumanity, they will react with inhumanity, and if you want proof of that just look at modern Israel.'

There were some mutterings around him. One of the other academics, an older man wearing a bow tie, turned to address him, 'I am fully aware, sir, that in British universities you are required to bow down before the Golden Calf of Anti-Zionism, but here in the USA we do not take such a blinkered view. The population of Israel is about eight million, and they are surrounded by over 400 million Arabs, most of whom want to drive them into the sea. So perhaps the odd peremptory action can be forgiven.'

Spencer dwelt on the casual but layered brilliance of the 'Golden Calf of Anti-Zionism'. If you find the right ringing phrase, any pompous bullshit will be accepted as wisdom. Was it worth carrying on with this?

He spoke, 'Do you have any idea how many Palestinians have been killed by these "peremptory actions"'?

'Regrettably,' replied the man, 'Most regrettably, anti-Zionism is almost always a cloak for anti-Semitism.'

There were noises of assent all around.

Walking to his office, Spencer reflected on how a person can transform from gentile to Jew to card-carrying Nazi in the space of a week.

He sat down at his desk and looked at the pile of students' papers in front of him. The pile of papers looked back at him like an unblinking and noisome toad. He hated giving grades because he knew that a poor grade could have a negative effect, not just on students' academic journeys but on their future professional lives. He was also not prepared to give a good grade for work that was half-baked and badly written.

He picked up the first paper. It was from a student called Donna, who had uttered not a word during discussion in class. He read it through and stared out of the window aghast. The paper was a literate and well-researched treatment of the topic, taking in modern critical theory but also quoting critics going back beyond 1900. The tone was balanced, scholarly and displayed an enthusiasm for Shakespeare's work that had never surfaced in class. He read through the second, third and fourth papers, and although there was some unevenness in the level of research and citation they were all well-written and very intelligent accounts of the topic, all displaying an impressive willingness to recognise the validity of different points of view.

Spencer did not know whether to laugh or to cry.

****

Spencer was jerked from sleep by the phone. He fumbled for it on the table next to the bed and heard it fall on the floor. He switched on the light, found the phone, and answered, 'Hello, Spencer Leyton, who is this?'

Jessica was sobbing at the other end of the phone.

'Jessica, what is it? What's wrong?'

She sobbed, trying to speak. Eventually he could make out her words, 'He's been here. He's been here tonight.'

'Okay Jessica, look, I'm coming over. I'll be there in five minutes.'

When he arrived at Jessica's house he found her sitting up in bed, covering her face with her hands. He held her for a long time. Her breathing steadied.

'What happened?' he asked, finally.

'He was here again tonight. He came last year. I thought that was the last of him, but no, he's back.'

'*Who*?'

'The man.'

'What man?'

'I don't know who the hell he is. I woke up and he was standing at the end of the bed. I could hear him breathing. Oh my God…'

She began to cry again. Spencer held her close. 'You say he's been here before?'

'It happened a year ago. He came three times in the space of a month – just the same thing, at the end of the bed. Then it stopped. Now he's back.'

'Did you call the police?'

'Of course I called the police. They were no fucking use. One of them kept asking me if I'd been involved in the protests against police racism that we had going on last year. It was pretty obvious that he didn't want to help me.'

'Jesus!'

'I saw a detective eventually. He said he didn't have the officers available to park outside my house every day of the year. He said he couldn't keep watch on everyone in town. I asked him what he advised me to do. He told me to buy a gun.'

'Are you kidding me?'

'That's what he said.'

'Sweetheart, try to go back to sleep.'

Fully clothed, Spencer lay beside her. Eventually, she drifted into sleep. Spencer got up from the bed and sat in the chair on the other side of the room. He tried to make sense of it all. If the intruder was the same man who had crept in last year, then surely he could assume that this was not prompted by his own relationship with Jessica and was presumably not connected to the attack in Greensburg before the gig? The intruder was just some creep acting alone rather than a member of a racist group – which was slightly reassuring.

He watched Jessica sleep and thought of home. He lived in one of the world's largest cities, but there seemed to be more lurking under the surface of this small town than there was in London.

****

They clambered out of the car and walked toward the storefront. A huge sign above the door read 'McKinley's Emporium'. Underneath, in smaller letters, it read 'Liquor and Guns', and above it all flapped the flag of the Confederacy.

'We can still back out of this, you know' said Spencer.

'I want to buy a gun,' replied Jessica shortly

They pushed the door open and entered the store.

'It sure does feel kinda white in here,' muttered Jessica as they crossed the floor, and indeed Spencer could see that there were some fifteen people in the store, customers and workforce – every one of them a white man aged over thirty-five. The temperature dropped at the sight of Spencer with a black woman on his arm.

One side of the store was given over to a vast array of Bourbons and American Beers. The other side held an even vaster array of guns. There were some accessories on sale: baseball caps, T-shirts, belt-buckles. Spencer glanced at the logos on display. There was the Confederate Cross intertwined with the words 'Hell, no, I ain't forgettin'; there was a pistol emblazoned with 'Why press 911...when you could squeeze 9mm'; the back of a T-shirt read: 'Keep Calm and Carry Guns'.

At the counter was a grey-haired man wearing a side-arm and a badge saying 'Hump McKinley – Proprietor'.

'How y'all doin?' he said, addressing Spencer.

'We're fine, thank you', said Jessica, 'and I want to buy a gun.'

There was the tiniest reluctance as he shifted his gaze from Spencer to the black woman.

'Look,' said Spencer, 'this woman is blind and…'

'Well goddammit, and there's me thinking that white stick was for conducting an orchestra.'

'I have told her that it's insane to think that she could buy a gun.'

Hump Mckinley looked him in the eye and spoke the words Spencer had been waiting to hear since arriving in the South: 'You're not from round here, are yuh?'

Jessica spoke up, 'Don't mind him. He's not familiar with the way we do things.'

A customer wearing a National Rifle Association baseball cap had joined them: 'Where're you from, anyways?'

'I'm from London.'

'Is that London, England?'

'Yep.'

'Is that the place where y'all elected a Muslim as Mayor?'

Spencer grunted assent.

'Well my English friend, over here we have not yet given up and rolled over on our backs. Not yet.'

Spencer turned back to the proprietor, 'I do realise we are wasting your time, but she insisted on coming here. I'm sorry.'

Hump gave his professional judgement, 'If I refused to sell a gun to a blind person, I would be contravening the Americans with Disabilities Act. Maybe over there in England it's okay to discriminate against blind people, but over here it's not. No sir.' He turned back to his customer, 'And what would you be thinking of doing with this gun, ma'am?'

'Well, shooting at people obviously,' yelped an exasperated Spencer, 'Has this entire country gone mad?'

'Perhaps,' said Jessica in a summoning-up-her-dignity voice, 'you will let me answer the gentleman for myself. I am truly sorry Mr… er …'

'Oh, you can call me Hump.'

'I am obliged to you… Hump.' Was it just his imagination or could Spencer hear something of Blanche Dubois creeping into Jessica's voice?

'You see, Ma'am, if you want the gun for concealed carry, then you will need a licence I'm afraid…'

'Oh no, I just need the gun at home.'

'Are you sure? Many of my blind customers find it reassuring to carry a gun when they're out and about, at the workplace, at the shopping mall...'

Spencer exploded, '"Many of my blind customers?" My God, how many do you have?'

Suddenly he had a mental image of a shopping mall full of blind people firing handguns. 'For God sake, how is anyone left alive?'

His eye was caught by what seemed to be a military assault rifle hanging on the wall behind the counter. 'Excuse me,' he said, pointing up at it, 'but what is that there?'

'I am not convinced that you are a serious customer, sir, but since you ask, that is an AR-15 style carbine. You would need about a thousand dollars for one of those.'

'But it's a machine gun, isn't it?'

'Well, it's a semi-automatic rifle.'

'And what would that be used for?'

'Oh… hunting deer.'

'How many bullets does it hold?'

'It comes with a magazine of thirty rounds.'

'*Thirty?* Is that in case the deer starts shooting back?'

'Forgive me, Hump,' intoned Jessica/Blanche, 'I am afraid I have only myself to blame… you see, this is what happens when you hire a foreigner as a driver. Next time I shall know better. Next time I shall hire American.'

This was greeted with whoops of approval by the other customers, all of whom were now taking a keen interest in the conversation.

'I must tell you Hump,' Jessica's voice dropped to a remarkable level of intimacy and trust. Hump leaned forward over the counter nodding empathetically, the paragon of chivalry, Sir Galahad in a Stetson.

'I must tell you that I am very concerned about home invasion… and me a poor blind girl on my own.'

'Well, little lady, I think we need to get this sorted out as soon as we can,' said a determined Hump. 'Let's take a look at some guns.' He placed a lethal-looking piece on the counter.

'This is a popular line, and quite economical. The Ruger LC9 is a light 9mm automatic pistol. It carries seven shots in the clip, and one in the chamber – that is, if you were crazy enough to carry one in the chamber!'

Jessica joined in the guffaws of the other customers at the idea of the kind of dumbass who would carry one in the chamber.

One of the group – a tattooed Sir Lancelot – stepped forward with a suggestion. 'Pardon me Hump, but maybe a revolver would be the solution here. Y'know an automatic pistol can jam, and the idea of a poor blind lady trying to clear a jammed pistol while the bad guys are breaking into her house… well, that's a nightmare scenario.'

The other customers nodded sagely at this wisdom. Spencer, though, still felt that the nightmare scenario involved a group of homicidal blind people blasting their way through Walmart.

'Good thinking, Ethan,' pronounced Hump, placing a revolver on the counter. 'This is a very nice gun: the Smith & Wesson 642 Ladysmith. It's a 38 calibre and I would, of course, recommend hollow-point bullets. They expand on contact – causes much more tissue damage and blood loss. I can let you have this gun for $450, and just because it's you little lady… I am going to throw in a box of ammo for free.' With a cheeky, if bashful, smile and a flourish, Hump Mckinley placed the box of hollow-point bullets on the counter. The assembled customers burst into applause. Spencer had seen men flirt with flowers and chocolates but not with an object that would maximise tissue damage and blood loss.

'Well ma'am…'

'Oh, Jessica, if you please.' Her tone was somewhere between coquettish and simpering.

'Well Jessica, please allow me to help you fill out this form. Then we'll get you a cup of the best coffee in the state and you can take a real comfy chair over in the corner while we run a background check, and with any luck you'll be out of here in thirty minutes.'

'Thank you so much, Hump,' said Jessica, revelling in her newly found role of Southern Belle, 'and, if I may, I would like to thank you in my own way. You see, I am – in a small way you understand – something of a singer, so if I may… *Oh say can you see…*' As her voice soared through The Star-Spangled banner, every man in the room removed his hat and placed it before a chest bursting with pride. Every man except Spencer, who was creeping towards the door.

For the first three miles of the journey home, Spencer reflected that he had never actually heard someone howl with laughter before. At four miles he had to pull the car over to assist Jessica, who was hyperventilating.

Spencer returned to his apartment to find a broken bedroom window. On the carpet, amongst the broken glass, was a brick with a sheet of paper taped to it.

There was a typed message on the paper:

Our Esteemed Doctor Leyton,

Your reading of Othello *should have taught you the foolhardiness of crossing the racial divide, and yet still you persist in making the beast with two backs with that appalling black communist. How poor are they that have not patience! But our patience is at an end. We do not ask you to leave our once-great country, but simply to sever all contact with the blind bitch. Like Gloucester, she can smell her way to Dover!*

This is, like Calpurnia's dream, a warning – and it is not the first you have received from us.

Desist! Or face the consequences. This is the Ides of March.

Regards, Parnell Prince

CHAPTER ELEVEN

Sergeant Pat Mooney studied the sheet of paper, holding it delicately between his fingertips.

'Of course, Doctor Leyton, I can have this checked for finger prints, but I would be surprised if it gave us any results.' He looked up at Spencer. 'I have to say that this looks to me like a student prank.'

'Are you kidding…?'

'It wouldn't be the first time… and, y' know, students have used this name "Parnell Prince" before. More than a few times as a matter of fact… yes sir.'

'What do you mean?'

'It's what you might describe as an urban myth. I mean there is no such person. He don't exist. It's just that some folks, y'know, they find it terribly amusing to use the name just to scare other folks. They make out there's this evil genius working away somewhere and actually it's a bunch of BS.'

'So you don't plan to take any action?'

'There really isn't any action we can take. Students can be pretty damn stupid sometimes. You just need to get the college maintenance staff to fix your window for you, and then forget all about it.'

'Officer, I have to tell you now that I myself have been the subject of an assault. I was threatened with a knife by people who made it clear they disapproved of my relationship with an African-American colleague.'

'And your point is…'

Spencer struggled to contain his anger, 'My point is… my point is that this brick… far from being a student prank… is part of a conspiracy.'

'Well Doctor Leyton, y'know this is the South, and things don't move too fast around here. I am sure there are a few individuals who object to fraternisation between the races, but I personally do not believe that the moon landing was faked and that 9/11 was a plot by the Israeli government, and I have actually had enough of conspiracy theories. Goodbye Doctor Leyton.'

On Thursday afternoon Spencer was in his office. He made a Skype call to his daughter Rosie. They had a bland conversation about her schoolwork and about the weather in Georgia. He so wanted to say more, but he could not. How could he say to his fourteen-year old daughter that he had fallen in love and was being threatened by violent racists? It was all too much.

'I miss you darling,' he said at the end of the call.

'I miss you too, Dad,' replied Rosie dutifully.

They hung up and Spencer stared miserably out of the window.

The phone rang. It was Louisa.

'Spencer, you have a student called Dani Brooke?'

'Er, yes. What about her?'

'She's posted something on the college intranet and I think you ought to see it. I'll send the link.'

Seconds later it appeared:

SHAKESPEARE: THE REACTIONARY BRITISH VIEW

A foreign member of faculty has taken advantage of our American tradition of free speech to make outrageous and offensive remarks at a rehearsal for a student production of The Merchant of Venice. *Sadly, this took the form of denying Shakespeare's sexuality. The LGBTQ+ movement on campus must stand firm. This is just another attempt by the cisgendred heterosexist patriarchy to destroy a Queer icon. On this occasion the insult went further, with some inflammatory anti-semitic remarks. We do not advocate a boycott of this person's classes but be aware that a British accent does not denote any unique insight into the work of Stratford's greatest (gay) son. DB.*

He called Louisa back, 'I can't believe it. I mean I just did not say that. I… I mean I am an ally of gay people. I used to have one of those rainbow badges. I think I've still got it somewhere. I am not a reactionary. I…' he tailed off, aghast.

'Spencer, I really don't think any of your colleagues will take this seriously. There are some students who just get obsessive about certain things, you know.'

'What should I do?'

'I'm not sure that she's broken any rules. I think it's probably best if you let it blow over. Look Spencer, I have to teach now. Let's speak later.'

Spencer sat at his desk, lost in thought. Finally, he realised – this had to be dealt with right now. He sent an email to Dani.

****

'So who is your favourite blues harmonica player?'

Not for the first time, Bernard was quizzing Jessica on her musical tastes.

'Oh lord, there are so many… I think I like Little Walter as much as anyone. I do a couple of his songs when I play live with the band, and when it's time for those songs… I don't know, it sounds kinda silly, but I feel I have to ask him for permission. I have a friend who is a classical musician and she feels the same way about Beethoven. You become a portal, a channel for something they created.' She dissolved into giggles, 'I really am getting spooky-dooky about it, aren't I? And me a god-fearing Georgia girl.' She picked up a harmonica in the key of A. 'As an antidote to all that spiritualism, here's a song you can play in church. You play this in first position and it's a very simple tune.'

Jessica taught the class 'The Old Rugged Cross' and then smiled at Spencer, 'Sorry, next week perhaps I'll find something you can play in a synagogue.'

'How about The Old Rugged Yarmulke?' asked Anne.

At the end of the class Spencer reflected that he had still not found a way to tell Jessica about the brick through the window and the attack in Greensburg. Was it simply that he did not want to scare her? Louisa arrived to pick her up.

'I'm taking Jessica off to my place. Some of the girls are coming round for a little late supper.'

'Right… er… see you tomorrow.'

As he walked across the car park, Spencer noticed a white pick-up with Alabama plates. The weasley man in the John Deere cap sat in the driving seat and turned his head towards Spencer. Expressionless, he stared through him.

Walt lived in a small house in a suburb in one of the more select parts of Merganserville. It was already dark by the time Spencer arrived. He parked the car, wound down the window, closed his eyes and for five minutes listened to the crickets and their soundtrack for the Georgia night. How on earth had he ended up here? What had started the series of choices and decisions that had brought him to this? As a young boy, had he ever imagined that he would one day find himself sitting in a rented Nissan in an affluent suburb of Merganserville, Georgia?

Walt answered the door wearing a Louisville Bats baseball cap. 'Great to see you Spencer, come on in.'

A group of men, all aged about forty, were sitting around a TV set watching a football game. They were all clutching bottles of beer and munching potato chips. Walt was nursing a glass of Makers Mark bourbon. Spencer accepted a Club Soda, and introductions were made. Spencer met Wayne (wearing an Atlanta Braves cap), Dave (in an Atlanta Hawks cap), Jim (in a Prattville Patriots T-shirt) and Travis (in a Dallas Cowboys Jersey). Spencer regretted that he had no garment representing Kettering Town Football Club.

Spencer had watched the odd game of American Football on TV. He did not really understand the rules, and the game seemed to him to resemble trench warfare. One side moved forward a few yards, only to be beaten back again minutes later. Then there were the frequent commercial breaks stretching out the time. For Spencer, it was a bit like watching World War I – and seemed to last almost as long.

'Okay,' said Walt, 'everyone's here. Let's play poker.'

They sat at the card-table and Spencer was given chips to the value of twenty dollars. 'How long have you guys been playing together?' he asked.

Walt answered, 'Wayne and Dave and Jim and myself – we've had a game going for twenty-five years.'

'You're kidding!'

'Ever since high school. Travis is the new boy. He came over from Texas about ten years ago, and we can't get rid of him.'

'I guess I'm here to stay.'

'Of course we do like to welcome the occasional guest,' said Walt.

'Never had an Englishman before, though.' This came from Dave.

'Well, I hope you've forgotten about that little unpleasantness back in 1776 – you might fleece me out of spite. You know what they say – if you don't know who the pigeon is after twenty minutes, then you're the pigeon.'

'Oh we're not out to fleece you,' said Dave, 'it really is just a friendly game.'

'Otherwise you could get the law on us,' laughed Wayne.

'Sorry?'

'If we took your money playing poker, you could tell the police.'

'What…?'

Walt gave an explanation that Spencer felt he had given several times before.

'Playing cards for money is illegal in the state of Georgia, and as you will have noticed, poker is played with cards. For money.'

Wayne added, 'There's a place called Albany down in the south of the state on the way to Tallahassee, and a few years ago some guys got busted for a private game of poker.'

'Yeah, that was a little different though, wasn't it?' said Jim. 'It wasn't what you'd call a friendly game. Apparently there was twenty thousand dollars on the table when the cops walked in.'

'So let's play,' said Walt. 'Travis, you've got the first deal.'

'Watch out, boys. He's wearing his lucky cuff-links.'

Walt grinned and displayed cufflinks decorated with the Ace of Spades.

The game had been going for ten minutes when the door-bell rang. Walt opened the door to reveal a policeman in full uniform. The men at the table stared in disbelief. Spencer's first thought was that he was the victim of an elaborate practical joke.

'Good evening, officer,' said Walt, 'er… is something wrong?'

'No sir,' said Officer Flynn, 'there's nothing wrong. It's just that there was a burglary in this neighbourhood about this time last night. Did you see anything? Hear anything?'

'Er… no… I wasn't here last night,' said Walt, 'not at this time. I was out.'

'It was at a house three doors down the street from here.'

'No, I didn't hear anything last night. I was out. All evening. Until late.'

Walt seemed to be trying to place himself between the policeman and the card table.

Spencer wasn't sure whether or not to start concealing cards and poker chips in his pockets. The other men all sat there motionless.

Officer Flynn peered round the door, 'Are you guys playing poker?'

'No,' said Walt, emphatically.

'Well, it sure looks like you're playing poker.' He wandered into the room. 'Two cards to each player, then three cards in the middle… it looks like Texas Hold'em to me. '

'Well, officer, when I said we weren't playing poker, what I meant was we weren't playing poker for money. Yes, that's right. We just play for chips. Don't we boys?'

The men at the table all concurred emphatically.

'Well, that really is unusual,' murmured Officer Flynn, 'do you just play Hold'em?'

'Pretty much.'

'You don't play any other variants?'

'Not really.'

Spencer, Walt, Wayne, Dave, Jim and Travis were all willing the policeman to leave the house and not return.

'You don't play seven-card stud?'

'Well, we tried it back in the day…'

'Do you play Omaha?'

'No.'

'Five card draw?'

'No.'

'Five card stud?'

 'No.'

'Razz?'

'No.'

'Pineapple?'

'No.'

'Lowball?'

'No.'

'Chicago?'

'No.'

'Cincinnati?'

'No?'

'Baseball?'

'No.'

'Follow the Queen?'

'No.'

'Shoot the Monkey?'

'No.'

'Fuck the Mule?'

'No.'

'Well look boys…' Officer Flynn smiled at the company and scribbled on a piece of paper, '…here's my phone number. If you ever feel like getting involved in a more interesting game, me and some boys from the station play most Fridays at my house out on the Parkway. Bring two hundred dollars. That should see you through. All are welcome. Except for those of the Negro and Mexican persuasion, if that even needs saying.'

The policeman gave a broad grin, 'I'm afraid I must love you and leave you. I'm going to get down to the Valley. I gotta bust another six niggers before I make my quota for the week – Hahaha. Good night.'

For a long time nobody spoke. Walt finally broke the silence, 'Jesus Christ,' he exhaled. The others shook their heads in disbelief.

'Are they all like him?' Spencer wanted to know.

'I'd say most of them are,' replied Wayne.

They resumed the game. As they played, Spencer studied the faces of the men around the table. What did they really think? In London he generally spent his time with people who had liberalism as a default position. His friends espoused notions of equality and diversity, not simply because it was expected of them but because they genuinely supported such ideas. In Georgia he was in a different place with a very different history. If the South had won the war, slavery would have continued far longer than it did. From slavery to equality was a long walk and he couldn't help feeling that there were still some steps to be taken.

Spencer remained cold sober through the evening and he played tight, hardly bluffing, and ditching any hand that did not have realistic possibilities. It was very different from the way he used to play. He assessed the odds of every situation and considered the implied odds. He quickly realised that Walt liked to bluff, and he found Dave and Travis very easy to read.

At about 10pm they took a break for pizza. Inevitably, the first topic of conversation was sport. After a few minutes on baseball, Walt saw that Spencer was being excluded so he asked him if he could explain the rules of cricket. Spencer observed that as a naturally irreligious nation the British had invented cricket to give themselves an idea of eternity. There was some political chat. All the men there seemed to be natural Democrats and the conversation remained resolutely uncontroversial. Wayne asked Dave about his new girlfriend.

'Is she old enough to go to a bar yet?' he asked, to laughter from the other men.

'Does she fit the formula?' asked Travis.

'Formula?'

'Yeah – you know: she has to be half your age plus seven years. Anything younger is off limits.'

'Who came up with that?' asked Dave.

'Well, it wasn't Walt 'cos he sure don't abide by it. Hahaha.' Travis laughed.

Spencer noticed Walt give Travis a very sharp look.

'Well, I've been single so long, I'd be happy with twice my age plus seven,' said Jim.

'That sounds like that hooker Travis went with,' offered Dave to general laughter.

Spencer could not resist asking, 'Sorry guys – was that a joke… about the hooker?'

'Jesus, Spencer – don't get Travis going on his hooker stories,' said Walt.

Despite himself, Spencer looked expectantly at Travis, 'Er, sorry Travis… is this the Valley we're talking about?'

More general laughter. 'Go to the Valley if you want a hooker strung out on meth. No, no… this was in Vegas last year. I was just curious, and I'd won $400 playing blackjack, so I didn't mind about the money. She was real nice looking and I paid for sex. It was okay, y'know. I mean I had a girlfriend back here at the time, but it didn't seem like cheating. It's not like an affair with someone from the office, is it?'

Spencer wondered if the girlfriend would have seen it quite that way.

'If you're going to the Valley take Walt along with his knife,' said Dave.

Spencer gave Walt a puzzled look.

'It's actually not so funny,' said Walt, 'but these clowns won't leave it alone.' He played with his chips for a moment. 'Anyway, I've told you about it. Back in the day I got involved in a knife-fight. I got hurt, but the other guy came off worse. I really don't need to say any more about it.'

After the break, Spencer continued to play tight, never chasing his losses, never taking more than a calculated risk. He played, in fact, like a poker player and not like the gambler he used to be. The result was that by the end of the evening he was nearly eighty dollars in profit.

Spencer said goodbye to his new acquaintances, thanked Walt for the evening, and drove off. He was driving home through the downtown area when he suddenly pulled over to the kerb. He thought for a while, turned the car round and headed south. He drove into the Valley.

He went slowly down a main drag that seemed desolate at night, and probably was not much more welcoming in the daytime. Most of the shops were boarded up and there was little sign of life. Some of the street lights were out and most of the illumination came from a gas station two hundred yards along. A drunken man staggered along the sidewalk. Another drunk was propped up against a wall. He could see a man lying in a doorway, burrowed down in an ancient bedroll on what was turning into a chilly night.

Suddenly, a young woman stepped in front of his car. He slammed on the brakes and she walked on, stumbling in high heels, oblivious to him, oblivious to everything. Spencer pulled over to the kerb and sat for a few moments, engine running. A woman appeared from an alleyway. She started to walk towards him, thin legs freezing in a short skirt. He touched the gas pedal and moved on. A young man on the corner watched him intently as he drove by.

Spencer passed the gas station and took a right into a narrow side street. He drove very slowly, then pulled up. He sat for a while, then got out of the car and stepped over to a man asleep on the ground. Long grey hair filtered out from under a Veteran baseball cap. He wore a naval pea coat that looked old enough to have seen action at the Battle of Okinawa. Spencer knelt beside him. There was the smell of skin that had not felt soap and water in months, mixing with the aroma of alcohol. He took the eighty dollars he had won at the game and tucked it into the man's pocket.

Spencer pulled his car out onto the main drag, and within seconds realised he was behind a white pick-up with

Alabama plates. He strained to take a look at the driver. Was it the man with the knife that he had seen at the Branding Iron?

They stopped at the lights and the driver of the pick-up looked to his right. In profile, it was clear that he was wearing a baseball cap. They moved off and Spencer followed, keeping enough distance so as not to arouse any suspicion. The pick-up headed west out of town, out onto the Old Military Road. After three miles it turned down a track to the left. Spencer braked, then crawled up to the track. He heard a dog bark. The pick-up was parked by an old farmhouse with a few out-buildings. The weasley man got out and went into the house. At the entrance to the track was a sign saying *MORGAN FARM*. On a rusty mailbox was a name, in red paint: *JAKE WYLIE.*

The next morning Spencer went to his office and opened up his emails. A message from his ex-wife Sarah came up. It was the first time she had been in communication with him for months.

Yet again you have fucked up. I have not received child maintenance this month. It is two weeks late. Do not tell me it is the bank's fault. Sort it.

'The problem is that it is the bank's fucking fault,' he muttered to himself.

A few minutes later he sat facing Dani across the desk. She sat with her fists pushed into the pockets of her hooded top. He had thought carefully about how to arrange the furniture in his office. He was placed strategically in a chair that was four inches higher than hers. He hoped this would give him the advantage without being confrontational.

'I take it, then, that you have no intention of apologising?'

'Apologising for what?' Dani looked up at him, eyes glinting.

'You have misrepresented me and insulted me.'

'No I haven't.'

'You have misrepresented my stated view and you have insulted me. Why? What have I done to you?'

'That's just it,' she snapped. 'On the surface you've not done anything to me. Underneath, though… it's a different story. You pretend to be on our side with your low-status teaching and your Mr Nice Guy act, but actually you're just the same as the rest. You wield power over young women and you enjoy it. I can take it on the chin, but some of the other girls can't. Teachers like you – you don't realise how much harm you do.' She sank her head in her hands for a moment.

Spencer was bewildered, 'I genuinely do not understand what …'

She met his eyes again. 'I'm playing Portia – one of the greatest parts in Shakespeare. I was longing to play it: a woman who achieves power in a man's world by pretending to be a man. I worked really hard. What did you say about my performance – nothing. Except that I looked ridiculous.'

'I don't think I said…'

'You just wanted to lock horns with the director – why? Because you felt threatened by a strong, intelligent woman? Or maybe the idea of homosexuality makes you uncomfortable? I wanted to make a feminist statement, playing this part in a way that I think serves the truth of the play and the author's intentions, and you had nothing constructive to say at all.'

Do we feel angry when criticism hits home? Spencer was starting to feel angry.

'Finished?'

'For the time being.'

'I really think it's a bit rich you calling yourself a feminist.'

'What does that mean?'

'How the hell can you be a feminist when you make your money taking your clothes of in a dive in Atlanta? You're a goddamn hypocrite.'

There was a moment of fear on her face, replaced at once by a slow, grim smile.

'And I wonder how you know about that? Have you been there?'

'Perhaps it's time to remind you that I am your teacher, and I don't have to take any more of your lip.'

Did he really just say that?

'I will not have a man lecture me on feminism. If strip clubs are so fucking evil, why were you in one? Would you want your daughter to be a stripper? No. But you like to *look* at strippers, don't you? I make money with my body, just like a ballet dancer or a football player.' She took in a long breath, 'My father fought in Vietnam. Fighting for his country and defending freedom – that's what he thought – well tell that to a Vietnamese orphan. So what's worse – stripping or killing? I want to change the world, but to do that I need an education. My father died and left us nothing. My mother lost her job. I have to pay my own way, and I make more money in two nights at that place than I would in a week waiting tables.'

'I actually think I've had enough of this conversation. I'll see you in class.'

Dani left the room. Spencer stood up. He needed to clear his head. He left the office and walked out onto the campus lawn. His phone rang. Jessica's name came up on the screen.

'I just saw Walt Hite.'

'Yeah?'

'He was talking about you. It seems that our relationship is common knowledge all over campus.'

'So is that a problem?'

'He also said that you and he had been playing poker. For money.'

'Yes, well, I think that is how it is normally played.''

'What the hell were you doing playing poker?'

'Because there was absolutely no harm in it. It was a friendly game. It was social poker.'

'Gambling is gambling, and you have to avoid it.'

'Look, I know an awful lot about gambling, and you don't know anything at all. I'm telling you there was no harm in it.'

'So why didn't you tell me last night that you were going to a poker game?'

'Maybe this conversation is the answer to that question.'

There was silence at Jessica's end.

'Okay, well I'll meet you at five o'clock at your office. Goodbye.'

Spencer walked on. He was angry. He did not quite know who he was angry with, but he knew he was angry. It seemed like everyone was out to get him. He turned a corner and there, lounging against a wall, in conversation with another student, was Theo Gustafsson. Both young men were smartly dressed in the preppy look that was favoured by the wealthier Pellier students. Theo glanced at him and then muttered something to the other student, who smirked. Spencer drew up to them.

'What did he just say?'

The young man dropped his eyes.

Spencer turned to Theo, 'What did you just say?'

'Nothing.'

'Well you said something because I saw your lips move.'

They stared at each other in a stand-off. The other young man stared at the ground.

Spencer stepped forward and slapped Theo across the face. Theo flinched, but stood his ground.

'Tell me what you just said.'

'Okay. I'll tell you what I said. I told my buddy here that I can understand a race traitor if it's for someone who is actually worth it. I mean, maybe if there was a really hot black woman who knew her place but, well… an uppity blind nigger – I mean, come on.'

Spencer moved a couple of inches closer, let his weight fall back on his right foot, then put all the force he could into the swing of his right fist, making contact with Theo's upper lip. The young man went sprawling. Spencer stepped in, thinking about cracking a few ribs. Theo struggled to his feet, wiping blood from his mouth. 'I will get you for this,' he spluttered.

'Well you can try, but after I report what you said I don't know that you'll get far.'

'Oh, don't you worry. I won't be going through the official channels.' The two young men stalked away, then Theo stopped and turned, 'and I won't be using my fists, I can tell you that.'

At the end of the working day Jessica was closing up her office when Spencer arrived.

'I spoke to Dani Brooke,' she said. 'I know her quite well. She didn't turn in some work this week, and that is unlike her. She came to my office an hour ago and she told me she was upset and confused about a lot of things going on in her life but she was particularly upset about a conversation she had with you. Apparently you accused her of hypocrisy because she works in a strip club.'

'Yes, I had a conversation with her because of a defamatory statement she posted about me.'

Jessica pulled on her coat, brushing off Spencer's attempt to help her.

'Her father's dead and her mother has no job. I don't know if you were aware of that?'

'Well, she said something… '

'What is she supposed to do? Women do not have men's luxury of choice when it comes to employment – did you know that?'

Spencer could feel the heat rising within him, and the fist that had hit Theo Gustafsson was beginning to hurt.

'Yes,' he said, 'well I heard a rumour to that effect… does that mean that if a student insults me from a position of total ignorance then I have to sit there and take it?'

Jessica locked the office door behind her. He followed her into the reception area at the front door of the block. A group of students were in conversation there. Two members of staff sat behind the reception desk.

'Look, Jessica…'

'No. You shut up and listen for once. Where do you get off telling a young woman how to be a feminist? And, by the way, if you're suddenly Emily Pankhurst with a penis, what the fuck were you doing in a strip club? Actually, maybe taking money off dumb fuckheads like you is a feminist act. Maybe I'll take up stripping myself.'

'Yes – damn fine idea. You could have a great gimmick. She was the stripper in the mask. You could be the stripper with the white stick.'

Jessica froze. Spencer felt the stain of the words on his lips. On the other side of the reception area, a group of students were staring. Motionless, Jessica spoke very quietly, 'Go back to where you came from, you filthy bastard.' She walked over to the reception desk. Spencer followed her, 'I am sorry, I am so sorry…'

She whipped round and yelled at him, 'I may be blind, but I can see a man's true colours when he finally shows them.' She turned back to the desk and spoke calmly, 'Could you ask them to send a cab, please. I'd like one of my usual drivers, so just say it's Jessica. They can put it on my account.'

Spencer stood for a few moments, the students' eyes burning into him. Then he left the building and walked home.

In a daze, he reached his front door.

He let himself into his house and took off his coat. He sat, switched on the TV, flicked through channels and then switched it off again. He went into the kitchen, put the kettle on the hob and put a sachet of tea into a cup. He turned the hob off and took a bottle of Four Roses bourbon from the kitchen cupboard. It was almost full. He found a clean glass and poured a drink. He went to the front door and stood on the porch, glass in hand. He stepped into the street and stared at the sky. The moon was almost full. He took a sip from the glass. For some minutes he stood without moving, his mind churning. He knew that what he did in the next ten minutes would decide the course of the rest of his life. He walked back into the house, put the drink down, closed the front door behind him, and walked to his car.

Jessica's house was a few streets from his. He had just a few minutes to find the words, the words that would save him. What was the alternative? He would never have this again. No one else could take her place.

As he parked the car outside her house he saw a white pick-up turning the corner ahead of him and disappearing. He knocked on her door and called, 'Jessica, please talk to me. Please.'

He pushed the door. It was open. He walked into the house. There were no lights on but moonlight was coming in through the window. He called her name and waited. There was no answer. He knocked on the bedroom door and called again. He pushed open the door and switched on the light. Even before he saw her he knew. There was an odour he had not smelt before. He sank to his knees. A long, low scream started somewhere deep inside him and forced its way up through his chest and out through his throat. Jessica was lying on the bed fully clothed with her eyes open. Her head was twisted to one side, with a huge gash in her throat. The sheets were soaked with blood. A pool of blood was forming on the floor. Kneeling, he covered his face with his hands and sobbed and sobbed and sobbed. He knelt and wept for minutes, months until he was empty.

He stood. At first he could not move and then very slowly he crossed the room. Every muscle was straining, as if he were walking through thick mud. He tried to avoid the blood – Jessica's blood. He reached the bed and kissed her cheek. He opened the bedside cabinet and found the gun and ammunition. He picked them up and took them out to his car. Then he called the police.

CHAPTER TWELVE

When Spencer woke, he did not know where he was. For a few minutes he thought he was at home in London – and then it began to come back to him. The flight from Heathrow. His job at Pellier University.

 On the table next to him was a bottle of Four Roses bourbon. It was nearly empty. Next to the bottle there was an empty glass on its side. He stank of alcohol. How much had he spilt over himself and how much had gone down his throat? It was only then that last night began to come back to him. Jessica.

He staggered to his feet and just made it to the bathroom before he threw up. He pulled off his clothes and stepped unsteadily into the shower. He remembered the police arriving, the blue lights of a crime scene. He remembered sitting in the back of a patrol car and then at the police station, answering a long list of questions. He remembered crying. And crying.

He was pulling on clean clothes when the door-bell rang. He opened the door to two police officers.

'Mr Leyton, we need you to come down to the station.'

'What, again? I was there for hours last night.'

'Detective Maclean needs to speak to you again.'

'I answered all his questions…'

'Please Mr Leyton…'

'Okay, well if I have to…'

It was only then that Spencer looked at the clock and realised that it was three in the afternoon. How long had he slept?

In the patrol car he realised that he was still drunk. Oh no… don't start crying again.

Captain Maclean was in his thirties, a tall, slim man with a well-trimmed moustache. He did not have the southern drawl of almost everyone in Merganserville. Where was he from? For some reason Spencer did not feel at ease with him.

'Mr Leyton… '

'Actually it's Doctor Leyton,' said Spencer, and regretted it immediately.

'My apologies, Doctor Leyton.' The detective was shuffling through a file of notes with one hand and tapping at a laptop with the other. 'We have been working on this case through the night and in the light of what we have discovered we need to ask you a few more questions.'

'Have you got Jake Wylie? Because he did it.'

'We are still considering… '

'You told me last night that the weapon used was a knife with a serrated edge. Jake Wylie carries a knife with a serrated edge. I told you all this last night… '

'Doctor Leyton, please… '

'He drives a white pick-up with Alabama plates, and I saw it at Jessica's last night.'

'Doctor Leyton, do you know how many white pick-ups there are in Georgia? And we are really not that far from the Alabama state line.'

'But you've got him?'

'We spoke to Jake Wylie this morning. He can account for his movements last night. He has an alibi.'

'What?'

'Officers were not able to find a knife with a serrated edge in a search of his property.'

'Well he's not going to leave it lying around, is he?'

'Doctor Leyton, we have to ask you some more questions.'

Spencer sunk in his chair. He told himself that he had dealt with this before. Both his parents were dead. He knew that the full force of grief could take a long time to come. He just had to wait for it to arrive. But it was not true. He had not dealt with this before. This was totally different from anything he had known.

'We have spoken to a number of people at Pellier university, and it seems that yesterday evening you had a heated argument with Jessica Murray in the reception area at the front entry to campus.'

'*What?* What the hell…?'

'This confrontation was witnessed by a number of students and by administrative staff… '

'What on earth are you trying to imply?'

'Doctor Leyton, this is a murder enquiry. I am not implying anything. I am trying to establish the facts of the case. Please tell me the reason for the argument between you and Miss Murray.'

'But this is a waste of time. This has nothing to do with Jessica being killed. I am telling you that Jake Wylie did it, whatever he says.'

'Please let me be the judge of that.'

'Okay.' Spencer took a deep breath, 'I'd had a confrontation with a student and Jessica disapproved of the way I handled it.'

'How long had you and Doctor Murray been romantically involved?'

'Just three weeks. Sorry… '

Spencer covered his face and went into a convulsion of sobbing. Even as it was happening he knew how theatrical it would look.

'It's okay, just take your time. Here…' Captain Maclean handed him a tissue.

Spencer took deep breaths. 'Okay, I'm okay.'

'One of Doctor Murray's neighbours says she saw you leave the house. You were carrying a gun. Did that gun belong to Doctor Murray?'

'Yes.'

'She bought the gun at a local gun store called Mckinley's. You were with her when you bought it, yes?'

'Yes.'

'The proprietor told us that you ridiculed the whole idea of a blind person buying a gun. Did you argue with her about that later?'

'This is crazy. This is just… mad. You're treating me like a suspect.'

Captain Maclean leant back in his chair, 'At the moment you're the only suspect we have.'

Spencer refused the offer of a ride home in a patrol car. He walked from the police station to his house, which took forty minutes. People glanced at him more than usual. What the hell did he look like? He had not eaten for twenty-four hours, but there was no hunger in him. His mobile phone rang, so he switched it off. As soon as he reached home he climbed into bed. He stayed there for the next two days.

****

'No, don't just have coffee. You need to eat something.'

'I'm not hungry.'

'I'll order for you,' said Walt. He spoke to the waitress. 'He'll have scrambled eggs, toast, orange juice. Thanks.'

'I've been trying to call you,' said Louisa, 'I left messages.'

'I've had my phone switched off. Is there any news?'

'There's a coroner's inquest tomorrow,' said Walt. 'You don't have to go. I'll go and report back if there's anything you need to know.'

'Thank you.' Spencer was almost inaudible.

'There should be a funeral next week. We're working on it.'

'Any word from the police?'

'Nothing official,' said Louisa, 'but Lloyd… you remember my friend Lloyd, the police officer?'

'Yes, yes of course,' muttered Spencer

'Well Lloyd has promised to let me know if he hears anything on the quiet.'

 'Thank you.'

'Look, Spencer,' said Louisa, 'don't worry about your work at the college. I'll take care of anything that's on your desk. Unless you want to come in, of course. You might. It might help. We cancelled all classes across the university for twenty-four hours but there's a feeling that it might help the students if we try to get back to normal.'

'I don't think I can come back to work just yet.'

'Well, if you change your mind.. . but keep your head down. The town is crawling with journalists and camera crews. We are trying to keep them off campus. Give them a few days and they'll forget about us and move on to something else.'

For a long time Spencer stared into the distance, unseeing. Louisa and Walt glanced at each other and sipped coffee, uncomfortably.

'What are your plans now?' asked Louisa eventually, 'I mean after the funeral… will you go home to London?'

'Well that's in the gift of the Merganserville police department. I might be spending the rest of my life in the State Pen.'

'No,' said Walt, 'there's no way. They won't charge you. They can't.'

'Maybe they should,' Spencer muttered. 'Maybe it's what I deserve.'

'Spencer, please…' said Walt.

'If I hadn't argued with her that night she wouldn't have gone home alone, and she would still be here. So it is actually my fault.'

Walt was starting to look exasperated. He began to speak, but Louisa held up her hand to stop him.

'Spencer,' she said quietly, 'when my husband was killed, I blamed myself. I felt such guilt for such a long time. Guilt is part of the grieving process: it's just something that happens. We feel guilty because they have gone and we are still here. You are not to blame for Jessica's death.'

'It may not be rational, but it is what I feel.' There was a bitterness in Spencer's voice. 'It may not be rational that I wake up in the middle of the night because I've heard her calling my name, but it is real. It is real to me. Please do not tell me that I don't feel something when I do.'

They finished breakfast and sat in silence. Louisa said she needed to go back to work.

Spencer and Walt sat for a while.

'I think we should go for a drive,' said Walt.

'Where do you want to go?'

'Nowhere in particular. Look, Spencer… In my experience, it's always easier to talk in a car.'

For the first time in days, Spencer smiled, 'So you don't have to make eye-contact, right?'

Walt laughed.

'Walt, I know you're not a great Shakespeare buff…'

'Well, not the way you are, you Limey snob.'

'There's a quotation from Richard II …

'*My grief lies all within;*
And these external manners of laments

Are merely shadows to the unseen grief
That swells with silence in the tortured soul.''

'Okay, so even back then guys weren't in touch with their feelings?'

'Whatever situation comes up in life, Shakespeare got their first. Let's go out to the lake.'

The two men spoke little in the car and took a walk round the lake almost in silence.

It was a beautiful day and the autumn colours were coming through strongly. Spencer and Walt sat together on a bench and watched the ducks on the water. They drove back without speaking. The stone on Spencer's heart had not lifted.

Walt drove Spencer back to his apartment. Spencer tried to read, but found himself beginning the same paragraph three times. He put the book aside. It was a kind of mental paralysis that had taken him over, and he had no idea of how to shift it. Would he just sit there, waiting for darkness to descend? If he tried to sleep he would wake soaked in perspiration. He left the house and walked downtown. It was lunchtime and the streets were busy. He stood outside the bank observing the people and trying to marshal his thoughts, but he could not keep an idea in his head for more than a few seconds. And then it happened. He saw Jessica in the crowd. She was walking, cane in hand, with people on either side of her. A cry came from within him, against his will. He looked away, shocked and embarrassed, as the people around him turned to look. His eyes raked the crowd again. She was not there. She never had been there. How could she be there? Jessica was dead.

He walked home and got into his car. For a long time he drove without knowing where he was or where he was going. On a long, straight stretch on the outskirts of town he powered the car up to ninety miles an hour and narrowly avoided colliding with a motor cyclist. He drove north out of Merganserville, flipped round and then drove back through the centre of town and out on the south road. He was slapped in the face by the hideous uniformity of small American towns. Every main drag was the same, with its fast food outlets and cheap motels, its car showrooms and gas stations, billboards everywhere shouting in frantic competition. He turned on the radio and put it up to its full deafening volume as an evangelist demanded money so that he could continue the work of God.

'Give him your money,' Spencer screamed at the top of his voice. 'He will give it to God.' He was laughing hysterically 'God needs your money. He's got to pay for the next earthquake; he's got to pay for the next fucking tsunami.'

At the lights, he wound down the window and started to shout at a man in a Toyota paused next to him.

Rick Mattani, a software salesman on a business trip from Durham, North Carolina became aware of someone shouting the words 'How the fuck did this happen? Why did you let this happen, you stupid bastard?' He looked over at a man at the wheel of a beige Nissan. The man was about forty, with wild, uncombed hair and several days of stubble on his chin. He was screaming at the top of his voice. His accent was unfamiliar. The lights changed and Rick Mattani accelerated away.

Spencer screeched into the car park of a McDonald's. An overweight woman in a station wagon chomped on a cheeseburger; in the back seat her two overweight children stuffed French fries into their mouths. Spencer yelled at them, 'STOP FUCKING EATING, YOU FAT FUCKING IDIOTS. STOP EATING. DO YOU THINK YOU'RE GOING TO FUCKING STARVE?'

He powered the car out onto the street and drove as fast as he could for three blocks, then slammed on the brakes. He slumped over the steering wheel, sobbing. He pulled out his phone, ready to call his daughter, Rosie. He had to speak to her, had to say sorry for all the mistakes he had made as a father. He clutched the phone and took a deep breath. Why did he have to phone her? It could only upset her. How selfish had he become? He slid the phone back into his pocket.

****

'At present, all we can say is that Jessica Murray was murdered by a person or persons unknown. You will be pleased to learn, Doctor Leyton, that you are no longer being considered as a suspect.' Captain Maclean sat back in his chair.

'Five days have gone by and you have done nothing.' Spencer was trying hard to suppress his anger. 'I am not a detective, but I know that every hour that passes makes it harder to solve a crime. Why haven't you arrested Jake Wylie?'

'Because, as I have explained to you before, we have no evidence linking Jake Wylie to the crime. You should be pleased. You are not a suspect. You are in the clear.'

Spencer stood up and left the room. Outside in the street he began to feel sick. He sat on a bench and tried to calm down. He sat for a long time and then called Louisa.

In Flanagan's, Spencer sat nursing a club soda. Louisa sat opposite.

'Do you think maybe I should get some professional help? I don't know if I can handle this.'

'There are people on campus who can help. I can put you in touch with someone; that's no problem at all. Personally, I would give it a little more time. After I lost Robert I talked to friends and colleagues, and that helped – and then I found that getting back to work was the thing that worked best. Of course, it may not be the right thing for you. I don't know. You can teach the *Hamlet* seminar if you would like to… it's the day before the funeral. If it turns out that you can't face it, we can cancel. It's not a problem.'

'Okay, yes. I think I should do it.'

'Good.'

Louisa looked down at her drink, 'Spencer, this may not be the best time to tell you this, but I think you have to know. I have spoken privately to Lloyd, and he says that unofficially the police have closed the case. They have no intention of finding out who killed Jessica. Too many of them were pleased to see her go. There may even be a deliberate cover-up. Lloyd thinks some of the police are connected with a particular supremacist group, and that they are the ones behind it.'

Spencer sat for a long time with despair wrapping him like a shroud.

'So what do we do?' The words crawled out of him.

'According to Lloyd, we should not do anything. We will be putting ourselves at risk. Lloyd is going to make sure that this case is handed over to the GBI.'

'The what?'

'The Georgia Bureau of Investigation. It's what you might call a local version of the FBI. They are called in for cases where the local police don't seem up to the job.'

'How long is all this going to take?'

'I really have no idea.'

'I cannot leave this country until we have caught the man who killed Jessica.'

Louisa looked down at her cup for a long time. 'Spencer… there's something else. Something was found at the scene of the crime and it was passed to Lloyd in secret. He thought you should have it.'

She pulled a small object out of her bag and put in on the table between them. Spencer looked down at it. It was a cufflink.

****

Spencer sat in his apartment, staring into space. His mobile phone rang and the message PRIVATE LINE came up.

'Hello?'

'Hello. Can I speak to Doctor Leyton, please?'

It was a woman's voice, youthful, with an accent he could not quite place. He thought it could be Texan.

'This is Doctor Leyton. Who is this please?'

'My name is June Barton. I wanted to speak to you about Jessica Murray.'

'Okay, look… I really do not want to speak to any journalists right now, and I would prefer it if you didn't phone again.'

'No… I'm not a journalist. I knew Jessica Murray personally. I knew her at the blind school in Macon.'

'Oh, I see. Could I ask… er… are you a blind person yourself?'

'No. I worked at the blind school, and Jessica and I were very close, Then she finished and we just kinda lost touch.'

'How can I help you?'

'Well, I just wanted to speak to you about your feelings at this time.'

Spencer's voice tightened as rage began to constrict his muscles.

'Er… okay,' he said. 'Let me ask you something. Jessica told me that when she was at blind school she used her first name. It was only when she went to university that she started to use the name Jessica, which is her middle name.'

'Yes, that's right. I remember that.'

'So what was her first name?'

There was silence at the other end of the line.

'Go on… tell me the name she used when she knew you in Macon.'

'Er… it was a long time ago.'

'I assume that you are now googling 'Popular names for African-American girls born in the late 1970s'. Is that what you're doing? Go on – give it your best shot. Jasmine?

Ebony? Or is that a little too stereotypical for you? You're a journalist and you're a fucking liar.'

'You don't have to take that tone. I'm just trying to do my job.'

Spencer switched the phone off and began to breathe deeply. Seven seconds breathing in, then seven seconds breathing out. He was determined not to go into meltdown again.

****

Spencer arrived to teach the seminar on *Hamlet*. Dani, Chantal, and Theo were all conspicuous by their absence. Mark was wearing a T-shirt with a picture of Andy Warhol on it. Nearly all the students had known Jessica on this small campus and they looked dejected.

'Okay guys, look,' said Spencer, 'people have said that the best thing we can do is carry on with our classes and try to get things back to normal. Or as normal as they are ever going to be. I think this is what Jessica would have wanted.'

He looked around the room. For the first time at Pellier, he began to feel warmth for his students as they all, collectively, stared into the abyss of grief.

Spencer started by establishing that the revenge tragedy was a common form in Shakespeare's time and that *Hamlet*

– the most famous of his plays – subverted the genre with a hero who seemed reluctant to take on the role of avenger.

'The ghost of his father has demanded vengeance, he is beset with opportunities to carry it out, so why does he not deliver? Why does he hang about for over three hours stage time?'

There was a long pause. 'Any suggestions?' asked Spencer.

Most of the students found it hard to meet his eye.

'You see, your guess is as good as mine,' he said quietly. 'I just want you to use your imagination. Ask yourself why someone swears to do something and then fails to do it. Why does Hamlet delay?'

'Because he's scared?' asked Mary.

'Well, maybe…'

'Perhaps it's because he's a human being.'

Spencer stared in disbelief. It was Mark.

'Perhaps he swears to do the right thing and then he doesn't do the right thing because people don't always do the right thing. I mean, it seems to me that Hamlet comes to a kind of maturity in the play and he sees that it really is not enough to sit around feeling sorry for yourself because there are times when being true to yourself means taking action even if you're not used to taking action, and you can't be like your father who was a soldier and a king because maybe you're not cut out for that, and maybe the society around you does not want you to take action, but that might be because something is rotten in the state of Denmark and there are times when actually you know exactly what you have to do, but that doesn't make it easier. It's just like… well, there are times to turn the other cheek and there are times when you should throw the moneylenders out of the temple. So you can't just sit with your books in Wittenberg university. You've got to do the right thing.'

Spencer stared at Mark.

****

Agent Jim Emory and Agent Barbara Connor of the Georgia Bureau of Investigation sat in Spencer's apartment. He had made them some tea and they sat holding their cups a little awkwardly. They were both in their mid-thirties, tall and clean-cut in business suits. To Spencer they seemed too large for the room. He had told them everything he knew about Jessica's death.

'All this may seem very strange to you, Doctor Spencer,' said Agent Emory, 'but in a town like this attitudes have not changed as much as they should have, and that sometimes includes members of the local police.' He took a sip of tea, 'I know there was a case a couple of years ago where GBI agents had to investigate the Merganserville police when they seemed to be dragging their feet.'

'That was a case where a young white man was accused of killing a young black man,' said Agent Connor.

'And how did that turn out?' Spencer asked.

The two agents exchanged a glance.

'We were neither of us directly involved in the investigation,' said Agent Connor.

Agent Emory cut in, 'We have been brought in at the request of a local police officer… '

'Yes, I know who that is,' said Spencer.

'… and he has been able to supply us with some very useful information.'

'For the moment we would request that you keep a low profile,' said Agent Connor, 'this is a potentially hazardous situation.'

'It was hazardous for Jessica,' muttered Spencer, staring at his shoes. He looked up, 'How long before you'll be able to make an arrest?'

'It's impossible to say at present,' said Agent Connor, 'please take my phone number and we will be in touch as soon as possible.'

The Episcopalian church was full for Jessica's funeral. A large crowd stood outside, the service relayed to them by loudspeaker. Police patrol cars were in evidence on the road leading to the church. Some of the congregation were there to say goodbye to a friend; many were there to remember a martyr. Louisa gave the eulogy and ended by quoting from Aeschylus, '*And even in our sleep, pain which cannot forget falls drop by drop upon the heart, until in our own despair, against our will, comes wisdom through the awful grace of God.*' The choir sang 'Change is Gonna Come' by Sam Cooke.

There were too many people there, thought Spencer. He wanted them all to disappear. He wanted to be alone in the church with her, then alone at the graveside.

Afterwards, Spencer was introduced to Jessica's sister as 'a friend and colleague'.

Anne, from the harmonica class, assured him that Jessica had tried to 'Repair the World', and that we should all follow her example. Spencer walked home from the church and wept.

CHAPTER THIRTEEN

The next morning Spencer was walking with Walt by Pine Lake. As usual, they shared it only with the Hooded Mergansers: there were no people around. They strolled for a while, with Walt trying to make a little conversation. Suddenly, Spencer stopped and pulled out a cufflink. It was decorated with the ace of spades.

Walt stared at it. 'Where did you get that?'

'It was found at Jessica's apartment after her death. Recognise it? What was it doing in there?'

'I went to see her.'

'Why? You weren't friends. She didn't like you.'

'I went there to talk to her about Marie Smith.'

'When?'

'That morning. The day she died.'

'And?'

'Look, Jessica was a figurehead. Everyone respected her. I respected her. If she got behind a campaign with Marie Smith she could really damage me.'

'So you thought you'd talk her out of it?'

'No. I went there to put my point of view.'

'And did she believe you?'

'I don't know. She listened to me, I know that… Some water had trickled out from under the kitchen sink. She hadn't noticed it… I mean obviously she hadn't noticed it… I took out my cufflinks, rolled up my sleeves and got under there. I just had to tighten up a valve. It was only when I got home that I realised I'd lost a cufflink.'

Spencer looked out over the lake for a moment then turned back to Walt, 'What happened between you and Marie Smith?'

'Since when is it any of your fucking business?'

'I'm trying to get to the facts.'

'Are you the police all of a sudden?'

'Why don't you just tell me? What have you got to hide?'

Walt glared at him. 'I took her to the movies…'

'Even though you knew that it was not appropriate.'

'… And I kissed her in the car.'

'Even though you knew that it… '

'I made a mistake. That's all that happened. For god's sake, can't you see how things have changed? This could end my career. There was a time when in this situation the older man was usually believed. Now the pendulum has swung the other way and it has swung too far, because now it is the young woman who is believed – every single time even when the woman is a liar and a fantasist like Marie fucking Smith.' He kicked at the stones by his feet. 'I didn't force myself on her. I mean I told you before how strongly I feel about teachers taking advantage… '

'Yes. I remember. You were really quite vociferous about it. The trouble is, Walt old buddy, actions speak louder than words. I think you're a liar. Have there been other young women?'

Walt stared at him. There was defiance in his eyes, 'I'm starting to wonder why I'm telling you anything at all. Who the fuck are you, anyway?'

'What about you and that woman Ellie?'

'What? There was nothing going on between me and Ellie…'

'Well that proves you're a liar because I know you were fucking her.'

'What gives you the right…'

'I mean, okay, I understand that Neil was shopping on the other side of the street, but I don't see that changing anything. And… I mean fucking another man's wife in another man's bed – how low can you go?'

'You really have got a fucking nerve…'

'Did you kill Jessica?'

'No! Of course I did not kill… '

'You stabbed someone in a knife fight. You could do it again.'

'That was a 300-pound Mexican who was trying to kill me with a machete, not a little blind woman. There's a difference.'

Suddenly there was a gun in Spencer's hand, pointing at Walt's face. Spencer was screaming now, 'Did you kill Jessica?'

'Jesus Christ! Why the hell are you pointing a gun at me?'

'I just want the truth. Did you kill her?'

'No.'

There was an endless pause as Spencer kept the gun trained on Walt's face.

'I believe you. I think you could do all kinds of things, but somehow I don't think you could kill Jessica.'

He lowered the gun. 'Get back in the car.'

On the way back Spencer received a text message from Louisa. An hour later they were sitting in his apartment. Louisa looked tired and drawn. She spoke, 'Lloyd called me this morning. He is very concerned about your safety. Have you heard of something called the Confederate Nation?'

'Yes.'

'Lloyd has it on good authority that they killed Jessica. He also thinks that there are people in the local police who are members of the group, or connected to them at least, and he thinks they are after you.'

Louisa paused for a moment, struggling to find the words.

'He thinks… he thinks you should leave town. He thinks you should go back to England. Agent Connor is investigating, but it may take some time.'

'You mean Agent Connor and Agent Emory.'

Louisa looked away. 'It seems that Agent Emory is off the case. The Bureau is overstretched at the moment, and Emory had to go off to a case in Augusta. A teenage girl has been murdered.'

'And this teenage girl is more important than Jessica?' The words were filling his mouth like glue. 'Was she white?'

'Spencer… please.'

Spencer closed his eyes and slowly shook his head.

'They're not going to do anything, are they? All this talk of the GBI coming in like the cavalry, but actually they have no intention of seeing it through.'

'Spencer, that isn't true.' She took his arm. 'You are in danger and you should get out while you can.'

For the first time in days, Spencer let himself smile, *'Hath not a Jew eyes?'* He spoke in a mock-theatrical manner, *'hath not a Jew hands, organs, dimensions, senses, affections, passions? if you poison us, do we not die? and if you wrong us, shall we not revenge?'* He paused and spoke gently, 'Louisa, do you honestly think I am going to run away?'

She smiled back at him,' I wish you would. I know you won't.' She thought for a moment. 'You have Jessica's gun?'

Spencer nodded. He pulled out the gun and put it next to him on the sofa.

'Okay,' said Louisa. '"Concealed carry" is an offence, and the police will be looking for any excuse to pick you up. Maybe you shouldn't keep the gun on you, I don't know. Keep it at home maybe.' She dipped into her bag and pulled out a revolver. 'Keep this in your car. It's just like Jessica's gun – it just has a slightly longer barrel. It's not loaded right now but it takes the same bullets as Jessica's gun. Okay?'

'Thank you Louisa. Thank you for everything you've done.'

'Actually, I think I may have to do a bit more… I have a meeting on campus in a couple of hours but we have some time. I'm assuming that you've never fired a gun?'

'Things are very different where I come from. I don't know a single person who owns a gun and, no, I've never had reason to use one.'

'If you don't know how to use a gun, then you're a danger to yourself. We can go in my car. Bring Jessica's gun and some bullets.'

Louisa drove the car up a trail into the woods and parked.

'Spencer, there is something I need to know. Do you want justice or do you want revenge?'

He felt like crying. 'I am so far out of my depth here… I'm from Kettering, for God's sake. What is justice? This whole place is unjust. I think… I think I want to find out who killed Jessica and then I am going to turn them over to the police. But if the Merganserville police can't be trusted, then I don't know…' He looked her in the eye, 'The gun is for my own defence, let me tell you that anyway.'

'Okay. Well, smart people do crazy things, but I have to assume that you aren't going to do anything crazy… Look, Spencer, we don't have much time, but let me run through the basic safety rules. First, always assume the gun is loaded. Second, never point it at yourself or anyone else until your life is in imminent danger. Third, keep your finger outside the trigger guard until you are on target and have decided to shoot. Okay, let's practice.'

Louisa took a plastic bucket from the trunk of her car. They walked a few yards away from the trail and into the wood. They stepped over a stream and into a small clearing. The leaves were beginning to fall. Louisa walked into the clearing and placed the bucket on a fallen log.

'Okay, let's stand about here. You are about fifteen yards from the target. I don't think you'll ever be further away than that. This is a double action gun, so you don't have to cock with your thumb – you just squeeze the trigger. My husband taught me how to shoot and the main thing I remember is that it's better to take your time and hit the target than firing quickly and missing. So take the time to get the gun up to eye level with your right hand – you're right-handed yeah? – and steady it with your left hand. Okay, that's good. Wrap the fingers of your left hand round your right hand just under the trigger guard. Keep both eyes open and get the gun's sight on the target. Now – don't breathe.'

'Don't breathe?

'Breathing in and out will make your arm rise and fall and your gun will float on target, so inhale, pause, hold your breath, and squeeze the trigger getting progressively stronger as you pull. It's a little like increasing the pressure when you're applying the brake of a car. Go ahead.'

For the first time in his life, Spencer fired a gun. He was shocked by the recoil and hardly noticed that he had, in fact, hit his target. The bucket was lying on the ground with a hole in it.

'Good job,' said Louisa. 'Now look. I'm sure that the people at Smith & Wesson will tell you that their guns can put the bad guy down with one shot, but that is just not true. There are too many variables. Rob, my husband, told me that one of the other cops on one occasion fired three shots from a distance of twenty feet. He hit his target each time, but the guy he was shooting was still able to fire back. So you fire at the chest and you keep firing until there are no signs of life. No signs of life.' Louisa looked him in the eye. 'The question is, Spencer, could you shoot another human being? I mean shoot with the intention of killing. Do you really think you could do that?'

'I'm sorry, I know I shouldn't be calling you so late in the evening, but I want to know why there has been no progress, because there hasn't been, has there? You just don't seem to be dealing with this…' Spencer tailed off.

'You can call me any time, it's not a problem, 'Agent Connor replied, 'and I can understand you feeling frustrated about this…'

'Can you? Can you really? I don't see how you can understand my feelings about this in any way at all. I don't see how you … I don't see how you … or anyone …' Spencer was crying.

'I'll be with you in ten minutes.'

Agent Connor sat opposite Spencer, who was clutching an empty glass.

'I'm sorry Agent Connor, but… '

'Why don't you call me Barbara?' Her eyes were a clear blue, and like any good cop she listened intently, displaying no emotion, but taking in every detail of the man in front of her. It was as if she listened with her eyes.

'Barbara… the worst thing is that I know that it was my fault.'

'Spencer, you've heard of "Survivors Guilt"?'

'Yes, yes I know about that, but this really was my fault. If we hadn't argued…'

He stared at the bottom of the glass. 'I know who killed her and I want him hunted down.'

'I can assure you that if Jake Wyllie is guilty we will arrest him, but we have to look at every possibility. I'm sure you understand that.'

'It is like being eaten from the inside…'

'Spencer… please try not to let him win. If he is filling you with hate, then he is winning. That's why you have to trust us to deal with this. Try to put the situation out of your mind as much as you can.'

'I can't.'

'I didn't know Jessica Murray, but from what I've heard about her I don't think she would want you to hold hate in your heart.'

Spencer said nothing. He had the feeling Agent Connor had expressed this sentiment before in similar circumstances.

'Also… and it isn't easy to say this, but in my experience alcohol is a very unreliable friend.'

Spencer looked her in the eye, still clutching an empty glass.

'You've been talking to the Merganserville police, yes?'

'Yes, that is how we start the enquiry.'

'And have they been cooperative? Apart from that guy Lloyd?'

'Not as yet...'

Spencer nodded, then sat in silence.

'Do you believe in God?' he asked.

Agent Connor gave a start. The question surprised her, but the professional mask barely slipped. 'Oh... well, here in Georgia you grow up going to church with your family.' She thought for a while, 'But I have to say that after the things I've seen in this job I sometimes think that if there is a God he stopped listening to us a long time ago... Do you have a faith?'

'No. It never made sense to me. Look... I don't believe in God and I don't believe in an afterlife, but I do believe in heaven and hell – it's just that I think we create them on this earth. I've been to both of those places. And I believe in redemption. I wouldn't be here without redemption. But if there is redemption then there has to be damnation. And there are some people who have got it coming. As surely as the dawn they have got it coming.'

****

In his office on campus, Spencer checked through student records. Every student's contact details and address were listed there, and he soon found what he wanted. It was dark by the time he drove out to 674 Washington Drive – almost the last of a series of immaculate modern white residences built in the antebellum style. There was a red Porsche parked outside. The neighbouring houses were in darkness, but there was light from a window on the side of 674. Spencer left his car and walked up to the house as quietly as he could. He peered through the window. Theo Gustafsson was standing in the kitchen talking on the phone. He was nodding and smiling as he spoke. After a minute or so he ended the call and picked up a tailored jacket that was hanging on the chair next to him. He slipped it on and took his car keys from the table. If Spencer were to act it had to be now. He crept along the side of the house and waited a moment. The front door opened. Spencer leapt forward and got an arm round Theo's neck. He pulled him back into the house and hurled him to the floor, then slammed the door shut. Theo was flailing on the floor and trying to struggle to his feet. Spencer kicked him as hard as he could in the stomach. Theo groaned and went back down, doubling up with pain. Spencer pulled out the gun and stood over him. He waited for Theo to catch his breath.

'Okay, Theo, you've just met your worst nightmare – a Jew with a gun. Now you just have to tell me who killed Jessica.'

'Please don't kill me,' Theo croaked. 'It wasn't me. I swear it wasn't me.'

'Who was it then?' said Spencer, who was himself breathing heavily and trying to stay focused.

'I don't know. Please… I don't know.'

'Now listen, said Spencer, 'if I think you're lying, I will kill you. It is as simple as that. Tell me. Was it the Confederate Nation?'

Still stretched out on the floor, Theo stared at Spencer, his mouth gaping like a fish.

Spencer kicked the man three times in the ribs. Theo yelped with pain.

'Was it the Confederate Nation?'

'Yes.' Theo nodded, his body twisting in agony.

'When did you join them?'

'Two years ago.'

'Did you tell them about me and Jessica?'

'Yes. But they knew already. People saw you with her on campus on a weekend. Everybody knew. You've got to understand. I mean maybe it's different where you live, but… '

'I don't have to understand anything from you.' Spencer's voice was steadier now. 'and all you have to understand is that I'll kill you if you lie to me.'

'I didn't kill her. They wouldn't use someone like me for that sort of job.'

'So who would they use?'

'Someone older, someone with experience. One of the ex-cons, I guess.'

'Like who?'

'I swear I don't know who did it.'

'So name some of the ex-cons.'

'There's a guy called Frank. He was in the state prison.'

'Frank who?'

'How the fuck should I know? We weren't formally introduced.'

Spencer kicked him again. 'Let's stick to the point, shall we? Who else could have done it?'

'There was a guy called Billy. I was scared of him. And there was a guy called Jake who always had a knife.'

'Jake who?'

'I don't know. He talked about Jessica Murray. He seemed to hate her.'

'Did you go to Jake's house?'

'Er… no…'

'You're lying and I'm going to kill you.' Spencer pointed the gun at Theo's face.

'No! He lives in a disused farm, just off the Old Military Road. It used to belong to a family called Morgan. It's on the left, three miles out of town.'

'Okay. Get to your feet, slowly, and do what I tell you. Good… now empty your pockets onto the table. I want to see your phone, money, everything.'

They left the house and went to Spencer's car. At gunpoint, Theo drove.

'Keep your speed down to thirty miles an hour, and if you try anything I'll kill you.'

They drove ten miles south and then turned onto a dirt track going into the woods.

After another ten miles Spencer ordered Theo to stop and get out. They had not seen any other cars for the whole journey.

'Keep walking up this track and don't turn round till I've gone. It will take you the rest of the night to get back to town. By then I might be dead. I know that nothing I say can change your mind, but you might want to consider the fact that being a member of that bunch of losers got you into this situation, and I could have killed you.'

Spencer drove back into town and found the road heading east. After a couple of miles he parked by the large iron gates at the entrance to the cemetery. The gates were locked, but he found a gap in the fence. He squeezed through. There were no clouds and the moon was high. He soon came to Jessica's grave. He stood for a few moments and then lay down on top of it, the side of his face pressed to the earth. He spoke, his voice quiet but firm, 'Jessica, I have to do this now because in a couple of hours I may be dead. So I have to do this now.' He took a deep breath and began, 'I, Spencer Leyton, take you, Jessica Murray, to be my wife, to have and to hold from this day forward, for better, for worse, for richer, for poorer, in sickness and health, to love and to cherish, until death and beyond. This is my solemn vow.'

He stood up, brushed the dirt from his clothes and walked back to the car. For the sixth time he checked that the gun was loaded and slipped it into his pocket. Then he drove off.

Spencer parked the car by the sign saying *MORGAN FARM.* A light was on in the farmhouse and the pick-up was parked outside. Gun in hand, he walked down the track. Suddenly, the silence of the night was broken by frenzied barking. Next to the house, a pit-bull terrier in a pen was raging at the intruder. Spencer scuttled behind one of the out-buildings just as the front door flew open. Jake Wylie stood, shotgun in hand, shouting, 'Who's there?'

'Drop the gun,' shouted Spencer, 'drop the gun or I'll shoot your dog.'

Jake stared into the darkness, hesitating. For a second, Spencer thought about firing a shot in the air to show he meant business, but then realised that the muzzle flash from the gun would reveal his hiding-place. 'Drop it now!' he shouted.

Jake put the shotgun on the ground. Spencer walked towards him, pointing the revolver. He arrived at the door, and Jake backed into the house. Spencer entered and glanced around the room. A standard lamp seemed to be the only source of light. There were two threadbare armchairs and a table with a half-empty bottle of Jim Beam bourbon on it. There were beer cans and empty pizza boxes lying about on the floor.

'Okay, Jake. We're going to have a little talk. Just take a seat.'

Spencer did not even see Jake's foot move, did not see him stamp on the floor-switch for the standard lamp, but in the next second the house was plunged into darkness. Instinctively, Spencer crouched down. He could see nothing.

Did Jake have his knife? Did he have a pistol somewhere within reach?

The dog had stopped barking. Spencer listened as hard as he could. If he heard the slightest sound he would fire. The longest minute of his life crawled by. How the hell had he come to be here? How could a university lecturer from the East Midlands end up in a pitch-dark room with a murderer? How had he come to be holding a loaded gun? He told himself to concentrate as hard as he could.

There was the clatter of an object hitting the wall behind him. He whipped round and fired – the gunshot deafening in the enclosed space. A moment later Jake's boot made contact with the back of his head and Spencer went sprawling. Jake's knees thudded into the small of his back. Spencer yelped with pain as Jake's hands grabbed his right arm, lifted his hand and smacked it against the floor. He felt the gun being torn from him. He froze, waiting for the bullet.

The overhead light was switched on. Jake Wylie was laughing. 'You're supposed to be some kind of college professor and you fell for the oldest trick in the book. I threw a bottle over your head you damn fool. Now you just make yourself comfortable. We're gonna have that talk you mentioned.'

Spencer climbed into one of the armchairs. Jake Wylie sat opposite, gun in hand. There was a long silence. Finally, Spencer spoke.

'You killed Jessica?'

'Yeah, I did, and I'm about to kill you.' Jake Wylie smiled to himself. 'At first I just wanted to scare her off,' he said. 'That's why I went into the house. Then I thought maybe I'd fuck her, but then I realised that the people helping me really wouldn't appreciate that.'

'The people helping you?'

'Do you think this was just my idea? They told me I had to find out all about her. And all about you. I found out who gave her a ride home, and found out when she was on her own.'

'So you were stalking her last year?'

'Oh, that was different. That was my idea. I didn't just call on *her* anyway. There were others. Not just here in this town. Then they said if I killed her they'd pay me, and they'd make sure I'd get away with it. And they have.'

Jake chuckled to himself, 'I thought maybe I'd gouge out her eyes. Well she wasn't using them was she?'

Spencer felt sick. 'What was the alibi you gave the police?'

'I told them I was here watching the football game on TV, and my people have lined up three guys who'll swear in court they were here with me.'

'Where's the knife?'

'I threw it in the lake.'

'Why did they want her dead?'

'You don't live here, so you won't understand. They're taking over and it's the ones like her that's leading it. The white man is already outnumbered – did you know that? It wasn't like that here when I was a boy. We had coloured folks and we had a handful of niggers.'

Spencer stared at Jake Wyllie in disbelief. He tried to remain calm. 'Really? And what's the difference?'

'The coloured folks know their place and the niggers don't. When I was a boy we knew Chicago was full of niggers, but it was different here. The coloured folks didn't like subversives any more than we did. Niggers like that blind bitch have changed all that.'

'Your country is founded on the idea that all men are created equal…'

'That's all white men you goddamn fool. The Founding Fathers were slave-owners. Do you really think they wanted to see a nigger in the White House? Is that really what they had in mind?'

It has been said that the prospect of imminent death concentrates the mind wonderfully. Spencer's mind was racing. He was not going to die in a squalid shack at the hands of a man like Jake Wylie.

'There's just one problem, Jake.'

'What's that?'

'The police are on their way here right now and if they find my dead body here with you then you're going to have some explaining to do.'

'You're lying,' said Jake.

Whether it was an owl, or a snake or a coyote, Spencer would never know, but at that moment something spooked Jake's dog, who erupted into furious barking. Jake stood and crossed to the front door. The two men were less than two paces apart. Jake opened the door and looked out. This was Spencer's chance. He leapt up, grabbed the bottle of Jim Beam from the table and with all his strength brought it down on Jake's head. Jake went down. Spencer pinned his right arm to the floor and began to beat Jake's gun-hand with the bottle. Groaning, Jake let go of the gun and Spencer scooped it up.

Spencer stood, gun in hand, breathing heavily. Jake raised himself onto his elbows and looked Spencer in the eye.

'So what are you gonna do now? Are you gonna turn me in to the police? You can't prove a damn thing. Anyway, even if you had evidence I'd still walk free.'

'I've got evidence. I know where the knife is.'

'Do you really think they'll search the lake? They won't bother. Anyway that's not enough. Hell, I'll still walk free. There's no way I'll go to Death Row. Not for a nigger. I mean I know she was a figurehead and all that bullshit, but even if you get the fanciest Kike lawyers down from New York they can't fix the jury, and I've got plenty of friends in this town. Lots of folks feel the way I do. The Nation will sort it out.'

'The Nation?'

'The Confederate Nation. Did you think I meant the Nation of fucking Islam?'

Spencer pulled out his phone and made the call.

'I could just take that gun off you,' said Jake, 'because I do not believe you have it in you to shoot me.'

Spencer stared at Jake. Was there just a flicker of doubt behind those eyes? Spencer thought for a second and then dug in his pocket for his car-keys. Still keeping the gun trained on him, he threw the keys to Jake.

'Those Alabama plates of yours are too damn distinctive. They'll hunt you down in seconds. Take my car and go. It's at the end of the driveway. You'll find a gun in the glove compartment of the car.'

'What?'

'You heard.'

'Why the fuck are you doing this?'

'I just want to give you a chance.'

There was the sound of a police siren far in the distance.

'You've got about two minutes,' said Spencer.

Jake stumbled out of the door and ran along the driveway towards the car. Spencer followed with the revolver in his hand. He could see Jake getting into the car, fumbling in the glove compartment and then turning the key. The engine coughed into life. Spencer took his time. He brought the gun up, held his breath and squeezed the trigger. His first shot went wide. He fired again and found his target – the front tyre. His next shot hit the rear tyre. The car lurched forward and stopped.

An unmarked car with a blue light squealed to a halt, headlamps on. Agent Connor stepped out, her hand on her gun. Jake stepped out of the inert car, revolver in hand. Agent Connor drew her pistol and shouted, 'Drop the gun. Drop the gun or I will fire.'

In the light of the headlamps, Jake raised the revolver and pointed it at Spencer, then lowered his arm and turned towards Agent Connor. He raised the gun. Agent Connor fired twice. Jake jerked and took a step forward, still pointing the gun. Agent Connor fired again. Jake stumbled and collapsed on the ground.

There was a long, long silence.

Spencer put his gun on the ground and stood with his hands raised. 'That's Jake Wylie. He killed Jessica Murray.'

Agent Connor knelt by the body, 'Well he isn't going to kill anyone else. That's for sure… Wait a minute…' Carefully, she picked up the gun and stared at the cylinder. 'It isn't loaded.' She looked Spencer in the eye. 'His gun was empty.'

'Well how about that?' muttered Spencer under his breath.

CHAPTER FOURTEEN

As with any similar incident, there was a police enquiry. It was officially accepted that Jake Wylie murdered Jessica Murray. There was insufficient evidence to link any other individuals to the murder. Spencer Leyton was deemed to be innocent of any crime. Jake Wylie's ashes were scattered at an undisclosed location.

Spencer dropped off his rented car and walked back into town. It was December and Georgia had turned cold. A large black Buick pulled up a few yards in front of him. A tall man in a suit climbed out of the back seat and a squat individual in a windcheater got out of the front. The tall man was in his fifties, grey hair swept back from his forehead. He turned towards Spencer and smiled, 'Perhaps we could give you a ride?'

'Thank you,' said Spencer, 'but no, I really do need the exercise.'

The squat man was standing in front of him. A gun occurred in his hand.

'We ain't asking. Get in the car.' It was the voice of a lizard. Spencer had heard it before.

'Or to put it another way', said the man in the suit, 'it was not an invitation so much as a command.'

Spencer was pushed into the backseat, the suited man beside him. Lizard-voice sat next to the driver. They set off.

The suited man gave a slight smile, 'Where are my manners? I must introduce myself. I am Parnell Prince.'

****

'I admit that at first I was intrigued when I heard that the appalling communist negress had got herself a white boyfriend – and an Englishman at that. I love England. Then I heard that you taught classes in Shakespeare and I could hardly contain my curiosity. Shakespeare – one of the peaks of Aryan achievement!'

 The room was a large study or library, the kind of room one might find in a country mansion. A hood had been placed on Spencer's head for the duration of the journey from the car rental showroom. He had no idea where he was, but thought they had driven for about thirty minutes. The hood had come off in the room. The curtains were drawn and there was no noise of traffic outside.

Parnell Prince turned away from the window to face Spencer. 'Could I offer you a cup of coffee? Or perhaps something stronger? I have a terribly good sherry available… too early in the day perhaps. Well, as I was saying… which is your favourite play? Can I shock you? I honestly think mine is *Love's Labour's Lost*! Hardly the orthodox choice, I know, but a delightful tale and a fascinating exploration of the use and misuse of language; could there be a more relevant theme in our own day? But I have to say that for me if Shakespeare is the Alps then Goethe is the Himalayas. Do not read a translation! It must be in the original. How's your German? I confess mine is rusty. It's seven years since I was last in a German-speaking environment. They say it comes back. I spent some time with associates in Munich. Learned people. I was engaged in historical research at Dachau and other sites of interest. I digress. You see, it just did not make sense. How could a man who would presumably agree with me that all the significant cultural achievements throughout history have been by Aryan men – how could that man be involved, and intimately involved, with a subhuman? With a specimen of the mud race? How could a scholar of Shakespeare be a race traitor? I wondered if it were the lure of the exotic. I thought, does her blindness bring out his protective side? Surely he could find an Aryan blind woman – he could phone the Foundation for the Blind. Well, I kick myself now, I really do. It should have been obvious, but – *mea culpa*! – it had to be pointed out to me.'

Parnell Prince was now standing over Spencer.

'And it turned out to be the same old story. *Die Juden*. Yes, our old friends from the Levant.'

'How did you know I was Jewish?'

'Because you told young Theo, and he told me. Bad move, I'd say. Anyway, every nigger-lover turns out to be a Jew.

You will never stop, will you? You will keep burrowing away at the foundations until you have brought it all down. Everything of value, everything that constitutes civilisation. I tip my hat. It's working. Topsy-Turvy land. A nigger in the White House – thank the lord he's gone. Our children taught to hate themselves and everything they stand for. You really are doing a good job. There's only myself and a dwindling band of patriots left to defend white women and children. You've been successful. You always are. The Holohoax – quite amazing. The greatest propaganda trick in history. Along with the myth of slavery, of course.'

'The *myth* of slavery…' groaned Spencer.

'Oh, slavery happened alright. It has happened all over the world for as long as can be recalled. It is very well documented that the Ottomans enslaved white Christians for several centuries. But the Middle Passage? The Great Guilt that white Americans are expected to feel? Well, let's just say that it is - to say the least – a massive exaggeration.'

Spencer's shoulders drooped, 'I'm sure you're going to explain it to me.'

'Do I need to bother? I'm sure you know more about this than you pretend. You people often learn the facts in order to deny them. Many of the Africans were paid labourers and were treated rather better than – for example – the Irish indentured servants who were brought in their droves. After the war they were worse off than before, because their employers had no money to pay their wages.

So Abraham Lincoln's war actually created slavery. But that doesn't play so well on television, does it? Watch a few of these so-called documentaries about slavery and when they run the credits you'll see the same names listed as producers and executive producers – the same as the names after the Holohoax shows: Bruckheimer, Katzman, Cohen. They are all there, raking in the shekels from PBS. Slavery was a fabrication to justify the aggression from the north.'

He gazed out of the window.

'Jews like you – you like to talk about genocide. Actually, the genocide is going on right now – genocide of the white race. But none of this can be said because Jews control the media. I am a warrior for truth while truth lies bleeding. Most whites know nothing of the truth. We are a breath away from defeat. But some of us, Doctor Leyton, are not going down without a fight.'

Spencer spoke, 'Can I ask you something? Did you always have this kind of hate inside you?'

Parnell Prince groaned with exasperation, 'Why does an intelligent Jew ask a stupid question? This is not about hatred. This is about *survival*. To survive we must let them know we are fighting back. And that, Doctor Leyton, is where you come in.'

Parnell Prince stretched out on a chaise-longue. 'Jake Wylie was a true patriot and his loss is keenly felt. The subhumans and their Semitic pay-masters are well aware of that, and there is rejoicing in the ghetto. They will clap their hands and laugh with childish glee. So we must send a message and let the smiles freeze on their faces.'

Spencer wanted to hit Parnell Prince. But he couldn't because he was tied to a chair.

'But where shall we hurt them? Where they feel most safe, of course – where they are enjoying each other's company without Whitey interfering. The barber's shop? No. I mean, of course, the church. How did he put it? 'Hoist with your own petard'. Actually, no… It's more of a two birds and one stone situation. A congregation of negroes and a Jew thrown in for free. Perfect! Let me explain how this is going to work. The Wednesday evening service at the Mount Zion Baptist Church ends at about 8.30, and all the negroes will be slapping each other's hands and milling around on the steps as they come out and they won't be paying any mind to the car that's parked right next to them. Then at 8.40 there will be an almighty explosion and anyone within about thirty feet of that car will be torn to pieces. And you Spencer will be the first to go. You'll be in the trunk of the car with a bomb strapped to your chest. You will be there before the service ends and you will have been lying there listening to them singing about how they want to be nearer to God and…' Parnell Prince sniggered, '…they are going to be nearer to God far sooner than they imagined.'

'Tell me something,' said Spencer. 'If you're an Aryan male who holds to the highest values of mankind, how does that square with murdering innocent people?'

Parnell Prince gave a sigh of disappointment. He shook his head and spoke.

'I wanted to meet you because I thought you might provide some intelligent conversation, but you're just as stupid as most people I meet. That's why I prefer to hide myself away.' Parnell Prince examined his fingernails. 'It's hard to know where to begin… you misunderstand the concept of innocence. They are not innocent, unless you regard a virus as innocent. Anyway, we are fighting a war. In a war, people die. In 1943, over the course of ten days, the RAF bombed Hamburg and killed at least forty thousand people – forty thousand civilians, people of their own race, fellow Aryans. Churchill was the war criminal, not Eichmann. Put the hood on him, Frank.'

Hooded, Spencer was taken round to the back of the house. When the hood was removed he found himself in a garage standing next to an old Chevrolet saloon. The paintwork was badly scratched and there was a large dent on one of the panels. This, apparently, was the car in which he would die. His mouth was covered in duct tape and he was strapped into a bomb vest: a fisherman's waistcoat with tubes of explosive packed into the pockets and wired to a timing device placed high on the chest. His hands were taped behind his back and his feet tied together. An oversize raincoat was draped round his shoulders and buttoned up at the front. Parnell Prince and Frank of the lizard-voice lowered him into the trunk of the Chevrolet.

'Goodbye, Doctor Leyton. I will leave you in Frank's capable hands.' The trunk was closed and Spencer was in darkness.

Spencer did not like lifts. He always took the stairs. To be confined in a small dark place with mouth, hands and feet constrained – for Spencer this was hell. Frank, at the wheel, took no account of his passenger's comfort, accelerating and braking hard through the journey. Spencer was thrown around in the trunk. It was hard to breathe in the airless confined space. He felt as though he were suffocating. He gasped for air. The journey seemed to last for hours, days. There came a moment when he wanted the bomb to explode, to blow him to bits in an instant. He began to sob. He cursed the people who had done this to him, cursed himself, cursed his parents for bringing him into the world. Suddenly the car braked violently and Spencer's head slid across the floor of the trunk. He screamed – a silent scream behind the duct tape – as something cut into the skin on his cheekbone. Something sharp. Spencer's mind began to clear. He began to take long, deep breaths, summoning as much air as he could. Finally the Chevy came to a halt. The engine died. Spencer could hear a small congregation singing a hymn. The front car door opened and closed.

'So long, Jewboy,' said Frank as he walked away.

Spencer rubbed his head along the fabric and found the sharp piece of metal sticking up from the floor of the trunk. It was a very small, jagged edge sticking through the trim. He wondered first if he could twist his body round so that he could tear through the tape on his wrists, but no – the trunk was too small. He brought his mouth to the sharp edge and began to rub the duct tape against it. He felt the metal tear through the tape and cut his lip. He carried on rubbing his mouth against the sharp metal. He opened his mouth as far as he could and slowly ripped at the tape. It was a long and painful process and he could feel the blood running from his lips. How long did he have before the bomb was timed to detonate?

Finally he had cleared enough of the tape from his mouth to make an audible sound. He took a deep breath and shouted as loud as he could, 'Help!'

He listened for a response. What was the point in shouting for help in a deserted car park? The congregation would hear him when they came out, but that would be too late. Despair began to swamp him again.

Suddenly, he heard voices. What sounded like a group of men were approaching. He started to shout, 'Help! Help! I'm tied up in the trunk of the white Chevy! Help me!' He realised he had not taken note of the car's licence plate. What if the car park were full of white Chevys? 'Help! I'm in the trunk.' The men were near to the car. 'Open the trunk! Please open the trunk!'

The trunk opened. Spencer looked up to see four men wearing white robes, their faces hidden by tall, hooded masks. On their chests they wore the familiar symbol of a white cross in a red circle. One of them was holding a shotgun.

'What the hell are you doing here?' asked Spencer.

'We're having a cross,' said one, 'we want to scare the niggers.'

'For God's sake get me out of here,' Spencer yelled at them.

The four men picked him out of the trunk and laid him on the ground. One of them bent down and untied Spencer's legs. 'Who tied you up? Was it the niggers?'

'What time is it?' screamed Spencer.

''Bout 8.30.'

'No. I need the exact time. And unbutton this coat, will you?'

On the lawn, some thirty yards from the church, the Klansmen had erected a fifteen-foot cross and had set fire to it.

'It's 8.37,' said one of the men, 'what the fuck is that?'

'It's a bomb,' said Spencer, his voice breaking, 'and it's about to go off.'

He struggled to his feet, but his legs, bound and motionless for the past half-hour, gave way beneath him.

The four Klansmen leapt away from Spencer and ran, robes flapping, towards the front gate of the church grounds. At that moment, Pastor Bill Green emerged from the church, his congregation behind him. He stood at the top of the steps staring aghast at the burning cross. Then he saw Spencer. Pastor Green and most of his congregation were within thirty feet of the bomb.

'It's a bomb! It's about to go off! I can't move. I can't get it off. Parnell Prince did this. Get back into the church and get onto the floor. Go. Now. I'm sorry. This has nothing …' Spencer began to weep uncontrollably, 'This is not my fault… this has nothing to do with me… Oh my God… Please just get back in the church.'

Pastor Green had turned to his parishioners and was pushing them back through the door. 'Get to the other end and get on the floor,' he was shouting. He turned towards Spencer and ran down the steps.

'It's too late. Just run. I can't get it off.' Spencer's voice was a cracked whisper.

Pastor Green turned him over onto his front. A pocket-knife ripped through the tape on Spencer's hands and then tore at the fabric of the waistcoat. His large hands pulled at the material, ripping it apart. He yanked the suicide vest clean from Spencer's body and hurled it high towards the burning cross. Transfixed, the two men watched it arc through the air and land on the cross-beam. It hung there, like the bad thief. Flames began to lick at it. Pastor Green pulled Spencer behind the car and both men hit the deck just as a huge explosion sent pieces of burning cross high into the air in a satanic firework display.

Spencer and Pastor Green lay for a while, covered in broken glass from the car's windows. Eventually, Spencer managed to croak a few words, 'Thank you. Thank you so much.'

'Do not thank me. Thank our Lord, for I can do all things through Christ who strengthens me.'

'Thank our Lord,' said Spencer, 'Our Lord and a pocket knife.'

Pastor Green smiled, 'Jesus was a carpenter.'

****

Spencer and Louisa sat over coffee. Outside, the sky was a December grey.

'Louisa, if they ever catch Parnell Prince… '

'You can testify on video, or Skype… whatever. I asked Lloyd. You won't have to come back. Lloyd says they'll never catch him anyway. He's got away with worse than this before.'

'Jesus… how can you have a place where some people are so good and some people are so evil?'

'Isn't everywhere like that?' asked Louisa.

'Frankly, I don't think so. God… I don't know. I'm just so tired.'

'When do you plan to go back?'

'There's nothing to keep me here now. As you know, my teaching's finished. I've marked the assignments. I was planning to fly back to London on Friday.'

She thought for a moment, 'Could you postpone your flight till the weekend?'

'Well… maybe. Why?'

'It's just that, well… I heard yesterday that some of the students and academics are putting together a memorial event for Jessica – a celebration of her life. It will just be a small thing on campus on Friday for the end of term, but I don't know if…'

'Yes, I would like to go to that. I won't speak, if that's okay.'

'Yes, yes of course… Good.'

They sat a few minutes longer, the conversation punctuated by long and longer silences. There was little more to be said.

He spent most of his last week in Merganserville on his own. If he had wanted company and alcohol he could have gone to Flanagans, but he stayed away. He spent much of the time listening to music, cocooned by his headphones: The Blues were there, as always, to soothe a torn heart.

Jessica's memorial was held in a hall on campus before a small invited audience. There were songs from the choir, some of them upbeat. There were stories about Jessica, some of them irreverent. For Spencer, though, it did not feel like a celebration of her life. How could a life be celebrated when it had been cut so short? For the final reading, Dani stood and read Prospero's meditation from *The Tempest*.

Our revels now are ended. These our actors,
As I foretold you, were all spirits and
Are melted into air, into thin air:
And, like the baseless fabric of this vision,
The cloud-capp'd towers, the gorgeous palaces,
The solemn temples, the great globe itself,
Yea all which it inherit, shall dissolve
And, like this insubstantial pageant faded,
Leave not a rack behind. We are such stuff
As dreams are made on, and our little life
Is rounded with a sleep.

Dani read it beautifully, with power and sensitivity. It was an offering of love and Spencer found it hard to hold back tears.

At the end, Spencer said goodbye to his colleagues. Louisa and other members of faculty all invited Spencer to return for a visit, 'When the time is right'. They all knew that the time would never be right. He left the room and found Dani waiting for him.

'Dani… thank you so much. That speech… it was just wonderful.'

'Thank you, Professor.'

'You really can call me Spencer, you know.'

Dani dropped her eyes and thought for a moment, 'Okay, Spencer,' she said.

'Which way are you going?'

'Oh… I'm going to meet some friends downtown.'

'Are you walking there?'

'Yes.'

'Can I walk with you?'

'Yes. I would like that. Er… I wanted to speak with you.'

They walked across campus on a chilly and darkening afternoon.

'Can I say something, Spencer?'

'You can say what you want. I mean, technically I don't work here now and so you're no longer my student. But I wanted to apologise to you anyway. I mean… that rehearsal for the *Merchant of Venice*… I'm sorry. I was really insensitive.'

'Well I was going to say that I was pretty rough on you. What I did… it wasn't fair.'

'You don't have to apologise.' They walked a few steps. He wondered what it was she wanted to say to him. 'And thank you again for your speech today.'

Dani walked, staring at the ground, 'I loved her. I really loved her. She had such an effect on me. I will never forget her. What she did… I mean, no other teacher… she made herself vulnerable somehow. She opened herself up. I don't mean she was vulnerable because she was blind. That kind of made her stronger somehow.'

A cold breeze was starting to pick up as they walked along the pathway.

'You know she taught the Reconstruction period after the Civil War?'

Spencer nodded.

'Well, she talked about how black people were cheated of their rights, I mean the tragedy of it and she was never propagandic or whatever, but she was invested in it through her own experience, and it made her a great teacher.'

'It's a gift,' said Spencer.

'But you see… I don't know how to say this.' She stopped and looked at Spencer. 'Why didn't you do that? I'm sorry, I shouldn't…'

'It's okay, really.'

'You see, I know you love Shakespeare, but somehow… you didn't let your passion through. You didn't share with us.'

Spencer was silent. He looked at Dani for a moment and then they both turned and carried on walking.

Dani spoke, 'I was hurt when you didn't talk about my performance as Portia, because acting means so much to me. It saved my life. I'm sorry…do you want to hear all this?'

'Yes. Go on.'

'My father died when I was young and my mother couldn't cope. It was really rough for me for a long time. When you're really poor – and I really do mean poor – it's all so demeaning. I didn't like myself for a long time. I thought acting would help me escape from myself, but when I started doing plays in High School I saw then that actually it's not about becoming someone else – it's about finding something inside yourself. I started to find some strength deep inside me – particularly when I played strong women. And that saved me.'

They crossed the perimeter road and walked toward the downtown area. The lights in the stores and restaurants were on.

'Are you still very short of money?' Spencer asked, 'I mean, working as a stripper can't be all that great…'

Dani grabbed Spencer's arm. 'But that's what's so strange. I mean, yes of course I do it for the money, but it has actually helped. I don't know how to explain it. It's the reverse of acting in a play because I wear a mask. It's a sort of trance. Samantha the stripper in the mask is not me. She's someone else. I don't have to go into myself – I become someone else. I mean, I'm practically naked, but as a person I'm invisible. I don't care what the creepy men watching me think about it – I feel free in my body at last.' She smiled, 'And I do get paid a lot of money for it.'

'Some people are going to criticise you for it.'

'I understand that many of the women I know would have a problem with what I do, so I keep quiet about it. It's hard to explain. I'm a feminist, and this is my choice. Well anyway, it's my choice at the moment.'

'I'm really sorry I gave you a hard time about it. I had absolutely no right.'

She looked him in the eye.

'That's right, Spencer. You had absolutely no right.'

'But we can part as friends, I hope?'

'Oh yes, why shouldn't we? Also…'

'What?'

'I didn't know about you and Jessica.'

'I thought everyone knew.'

'I only heard after she died… you were in love with each other?'

'I was in love with her but… I don't know. Perhaps with a little more time, she…'

Spencer closed his eyes and shook his head.

Dani took hold of his arm. They walked on. They were in the downtown area now and the streets were busy.

'The South has to change, I know that…' said Dani.

'I am not sure that this is about the South,' said Spencer, 'or about racism, or white supremacy, or whatever. I think maybe this is about good and evil. Maybe it's as simple as that.'

Dani looked over to a café on the other side of the street. She reached out for his hand and squeezed it gently.

'I'm meeting my friends over there. Goodbye Spencer.'

'Goodbye Dani.'

****

Louisa drove Spencer to Atlanta airport.

She pulled into a parking space and turned the engine off. They sat for a few moments in silence.

'Spencer, I think you know this, but try to hang on to the good memories.'

'Oh, there are plenty of those.'

'Do not try to move on. You will not be able to move on. Let this be part of you for the rest of your life. Jessica is part of you until you die. Live your life the way she would have wanted you to live it.'

'What would she have wanted?'

'Some of us can be heroes, and some of us can't. Fight injustice if you're brave enough, and if you're not, then at least take no part in it. Step away from it.'

They embraced and said goodbye.

Spencer flew back to London two weeks before Christmas. He had made it clear to his manager at the college that he was fit and well and would be ready to teach in January. Sarah had taken the children to stay with friends in France. He said he would see them in the New Year.

He turned down several invitations and spent Christmas alone. After Georgia, London of course felt cold and dreary, even bedecked with the commercial tinsel of the festive season. To his relief, Jessica never appeared to him in the streets. Occasionally, though, he would awake from a fitful sleep to hear Jessica breathing next to him. It became a reassurance.

Sometimes, sitting in his apartment in Clapham, Spencer would pick up his Lee Oskar harmonica and play 'Saint James Infirmary'. He was getting pretty good at it.

Printed in Great Britain
by Amazon

13596297R00173